THE PRESIDENTIAL SPEECH WE NEED

THE PRESIDENTIAL SPEECH WE NEED

Comprised of an essay,
a scientific experiment,
and a play entitled:

THE SEMINAR

Michael J. Weinstock

ISBN 13 Paperback: 978-0-578-59629-7

Cover artwork: Todd Hebertson, BookCoverArt.webs.com
Interior design: Creative Publishing Book Design

*To Charles Darwin, Isaac Newton
and Albert Einstein.*

Introduction

Ours is a history of ever higher perspectives; ever larger worldviews. We thought our planet was flat, but it was round. We thought the earth was the center of the solar system, but the sun was the center. We thought stars were uniformly distant, but galaxies raced away in an expanding universe. One day we may discover not everything has a beginning and end. But in every past instance, our well-being did not depend on adopting a new, and higher, worldview. That may no longer be the case.

Problems such as overpopulation, environmental degradation, resource exhaustion and growing fanaticism beset humanity and many believe the situation is hopeless; our problems are unsolvable. Indeed, they may be unsolvable if our vision remains static. But if it does not, if it can rise to a higher plane, where might that lead? I wanted to explore the question.

So far, it would appear that humans are genetically predisposed to ruin their habitat. Further, I suspect the constants in the universe, such as the masses of fundamental particles, are such that the kind of intelligent life they allow may not be able to evolve beyond its age of technology.

So, the situation does seem hopeless. But I also believe that, theoretically, our species has the intellectual capacity to safely secure its future on the planet if it finds a way to set aside its historical baggage: the belief the planet is ours to exploit, the conviction our current world view is sufficient, the instinctive reluctance to face reality, the innate desire to be led, and the primordial craving to acquire.

With all that in mind, this essay is just a thought experiment designed to address the question: "Though it likely cannot be done, if it could be done, what would it take?"

I set myself three goals in trying to answer that question: to make my case as succinctly as possible, to let logic lead where it may regardless of political correctness, and to provide solutions, not just identify problems. The reader will decide if I met those goals.

I also determined that the best way to identify problems was to try to measure the difference between the way we live and the laws of nature that assure our safety, and then to fix problems by offering solutions within our control. In the latter case, for example, I wanted to find a mechanism by which the people could be persuaded to break the gridlock in Congress, freeing them to fix four clear and present dangers facing the Union, allowing them to reorient the nation's participation in international institutions, and enabling them to adopt a fresh perspective on dealing with overpopulation, environmental degradation, resource exhaustion and fanaticism.

The mechanism I chose by which the people could most quickly begin the process of solving the nation's problems was a "how to" speech by the president, any president.

Michael J. Weinstock

The Presidential
Speech We Need

Dear Mr. President,

I believe events have conspired to give you a unique opportunity to set the country on a wiser and more realistic path, and to accomplish that I recommend you give the following speech on the campaign trail as the next election approaches:

"My fellow Americans. I have come here today to ask you to join me in a unique political experiment designed to help the country solve some of its most pressing problems. Before

I describe the experiment, I will identify the problems and describe a new way of thinking about them. Most importantly, keep in mind that if you are unhappy with the results of the experiment you can easily change them in future elections.

"I will describe problems and solutions as though they were certainties when in fact they are only opinions with which reasonable people may disagree. I admit this readily because that is what we do — we try to extract meaning from the world around us and often reach different conclusions. I will also employ very long-term and very large-scale points of view in the hope those perspectives might provide useful guidance for today.

"It is my opinion and heartfelt belief that the problems I identify not only exist but their existence is based on fact. And if they exist, to whatever degree, we should address them and not play Russian roulette with our future: as, for example, by blindly relying on technology to save us from climate change at the eleventh hour.

"This new way of thinking requires us to listen more carefully to what nature is telling us about our existence, our place in the universe if you will, and what lessons we should derive to live in harmony with its laws; particularly since they are immutable and unforgiving.

"We appear to live in a universe born about 13.8 billion years ago in the Big Bang. As the universe expanded and cooled, light was released to stream toward our eyes even though we would not exist for many billions of years. Since that time stars, galaxies and planets have formed and hydrogen and helium have evolved into the myriad elements we recognize today. As far as we know, human beings represent the most complex arrangement of those elements to date: blindly stitched together by evolution, blindly following the laws of nature.

"Whether that universe was set in motion by a quantum emergence, a multiverse, a Big Crunch, or some other agency, it seems clear that humans are an infinitesimal, unimportant speck in an indifferent universe and that their survival depends on acceptance of that reality.

"Our own eyes tell us the only thing in the solar system that cares about us is us. The Earth, for example, does not care what is on its surface, and all the other planets and moons in the solar system attest to that. This is probably true for all of space. So, if there are solutions to our problems they must come from us, for us, and for all the other species we have placed in harm's way.

"This then raises the questions: Why reorient our thinking? Why embrace our insignificance and possible temporariness? Why develop 'Cosmic Awareness' if you will? Because that way lies hope: because one cannot fix problems without admitting truths. One truth might be that humanity's most significant contribution to evolution will, in the end, be nothing more than the transfer of the fossil fuels of the earth from the ground to the air. Another truth might be that humans as evolved are fated to be an interim species; else why would their technology have gotten so far ahead of their enlightenment? Another truth might be that humans, the most adaptable species on the planet, are simply ill equipped conceptually and psychologically to adapt to the storm that is coming.

"That storm began gathering at the start of the Industrial Revolution when man declared war on the discomforts and inconveniences of nature. Had we been able to hear Nature speak at the time, we might have heard, 'You're kidding, right?'

"We now know the planet has limits and never before have so many people been in harm's way; never before in perhaps three million years have temperatures risen so fast even taking into account random pauses in warming; never before have humans engaged in such an existential, planet-wide experiment that could redound catastrophically to their detriment. Basically, the human business model has changed. We can no longer migrate, hunt, gather, fish, sow, reap, build, produce, reproduce and exploit without limit or consequence.

"Indeed, many biologists believe that, absent a massive asteroid strike or tremendous geological activity, humans will be the cause of the sixth mass extinction event on earth in the last 450 million years.

"Why all this background? Because the possibility exists that in the next one hundred to one thousand years the combination of human overpopulation, environmental degradation and resource exhaustion will cause a massive kill-back of species on this planet; including our own. I speak of kill-back, not extinction, though many species will indeed go extinct. No one can predict who or what will survive in such an environment. Perhaps there are genetic mutations that have occurred or are occurring now in various species that over time will allow them to endure higher temperatures, consume less food and water, and breathe higher concentrations of carbon dioxide and methane. No one knows.

"This then brings us to the first reason for the political experiment I propose. If you join me in this experiment, you may be assured I will take the following steps:

"My time in office will be dedicated to increasing Cosmic Awareness by every means possible. I am not sure of all the methods that might accomplish that, but I imagine a free exchange of ideas in our schools, over the Internet and through the media will facilitate the effort. Hopefully, our scientists will join in, not just to heighten awareness of the cosmos, but to bring to consciousness the staggering inverse dimensions of the subatomic world and the endless expanses of time.

"On an individual basis, I urge all men and women to let the starry sky enfold them, to visit the natural wonders of the world to experience the awe and majesty of nature, and to place themselves in context from time to time by looking down at themselves from a mile up, then a thousand miles up, then ten thousand miles up, and then as far as the imagination can soar. Indeed, we have already sensed our capacity if not longing for Cosmic Awareness lying in the grass under a blazing night canopy, sitting on the beach as the sun slips into the sea, standing on the edge of an immense Grand Canyon, hiking above a lush river valley dappled with shafts of sunlight, and yearning for intelligent life elsewhere in the universe.

"Also, spend time pondering NASA's photos of Earth and its neighbors in the solar system; particularly the photos of the Earth and Moon taken from the orbit of Saturn that painfully inform the heart of man's ineffable loneliness in space. Indeed, with Cosmic Awareness, we would know that those on Earth who waved at the camera when the photos from Saturn were taken, could just as easily have been waving goodbye as hello.

"Consider compressing the universe's entire history into one year to grasp the immensity of time. In that scenario, if it were midnight on December 31st, and you could peer back in time, you would see Columbus one second ago; the first anatomically correct human six minutes ago; an ape at 10:15 this morning; a bird on December 27th; a mammal on December 25th; a dinosaur on December 24th; an insect on December 21st; a fish on December 20th; a land plant on December 18th; a multi-cellular organism in November; a single-celled organism in September; our solar system in August; the Milky Way in March; and the Big Bang on January first.

"Acknowledge that we have one of the more pedestrian view seats in the theater of the universe. When we look at the night sky we are stunned by a spectacular profusion of stars, gas and dust, but they pale in comparison to the views of other entities sharing our cosmos. If you want to see what the night sky looks like from an asteroid racing past an exploding star, or from a rogue planet transiting above the disc of the Milky Way, or from a Jupiter-size planet orbiting near the galactic center, take a look at 'The Zoomable Universe' by Caleb Sharf, with illustrations by Ron Miller.

"Also, pay more attention to the messages we get from Nature every day reminding us of the terrible fragility, and ephemeral nature, of our existence. We know these messages as hurricanes, earthquakes, volcanoes, tornados, meteors, fires, floods, and tsunamis. To us they are background noise, but their more profound, underlying meaning must be made manifest. Indeed, in all of human history, natural disaster has been the only force compelling dramatic changes in human behavior that man was willing to accept with equanimity and resignation rather than rage and riot. Must we take that road again?

"Never forget that our uniqueness is a two-edged sword. However special we may be in intellect and achievement, we still 'take' (from nature), 'make' (into things), and 'waste' (in landfills and incinerators), while all other organisms contribute to the cycle of life in their birth, death, decay, regeneration and restoration. There is no waste in nature, yet humans are awash in garbage. There will be no sustainability for man without conformity to the circularity of nature.

"Acknowledge that we are the only species given the choice of consciously avoiding overpopulation, and our advancement of family planning and birth control must be broad and deep.

"Stop thinking of earth as a planet and start thinking of it as a lifeboat; a lifeboat in which ours may sadly be the last, great, irresponsible generation to task the planet before the tipping point.

"Recognize that we are at war with an enemy we have faced before, but not with such dire consequences because this time our civilization hangs in the balance. We are at war with ourselves and 200,000 years of genetic compulsion, only now we have to change how we think in order to know how to act.

"Acknowledge that our egocentricity, our obsession with ourselves, our total preoccupation every moment of every day with who we are and what we do to the exclusion of the wider world around us, is the ultimate barrier to Cosmic Awareness.

"Ask our religious leaders to de-emphasize if they will those aspects of the faith that encourage our egocentricity and sense of entitlement, and emphasize those that help us fathom our true role in nature and our responsibility for both the despoliation and restoration of our habitat.

"Recognize that the universe expresses itself in many forms such as space-time, radiation, galaxies, stars, planets, moons, atmospheres, continents, oceans, "life," molecules, atoms and particles, and we are putting at risk the form of expression that is us.

"And finally, take heart from the fact that there are people all around the world who have achieved or are achieving Cosmic Awareness so we know it is within the capability of our species. We call those people, 'Scientists.'

"My time in office will also be dedicated to establishing a 10-year plan to phase out the emission of greenhouse gases in our country and to minimize the chemical contamination of its lands and seas. The plan will prove useful in measuring the distance between where we are and where we need to be. It contemplates:

"Encouraging other nations to follow our lead, and our participation in as many international organizations as possible working to limit the climate change and contamination underway. Please note I am not so naïve as to believe the United States can do this alone, but perhaps we can hold the line in the hope others will catch up in time.

"The plan also contemplates aggressive legislation and regulation and funding to accomplish its objectives.

"It envisages educating people to understand that consumption begets production which begets pollution; and that the use of endless, mindless consumption and production as cure-alls for economic ills is self-defeating. As regards the preservation of a healthy planet, less is more. Further, a reduction in endless, mindless consumption and production will slow resource exhaustion and perhaps buy time for renewables to predominate.

"The plan also calls for educating people to accept that sacrifice is necessary to achieve the higher good of a livable planet. Developed nations must cut back on the standard of living they enjoy. Developing nations must postpone some of the standard of living they seek. Otherwise, we are just admitting that even if cutbacks and postponements are necessary, we would rather party on until nature does them for us, disastrously. Unfortunately, voluntary cutbacks and postponements are easy to prescribe but hard to do.

"That is why educating people about these realities is critical because the existential problems facing mankind can only be solved by insistence from the bottom up, not dictates from the top down. Cosmic Awareness can ease the journey, as can a new generation schooled in the religion of best environmental practices from childhood.

"Cosmic Awareness can also motivate people to use their most effective weapon against climate change: energy conservation. That effort might include turning electric meters at the home or business and sensors in vehicles into profit centers by incorporating personal energy savings into cap and trade programs; or developing affordable fuel-cell catalysts to make hydrogen cars available to the masses; or using big data to develop social-pressure-based approaches to encourage wise energy use.

"The plan also contemplates building up or over rather than out to preserve as much land in its natural state as possible; the strengthening and aggressive enforcement of laws prohibiting the exploitation of endangered fisheries and the pollution of surrounding seas; and the sequestering of 30 percent of the oceans into marine protected areas including those close to shore where most activity occurs.

"The plan gives priority to sustainability efforts in cities, and designing those efforts, in accordance with the circularity principles of nature, to maximize use of solar, wind and geothermal energy; treat waste as a resource; exploit the efficiencies of living and working in the same neighborhood; eliminate commuting time and transportation pollution; utilize rooftops for farming; and employ other available techniques such that incoming resources are designed for 'next use' and not 'end of life,' buildings perform the functions of trees, and public spaces become groundwater sponges.

"The plan also envisages worldwide efforts to plant new forests and regrow missing ones; to use compost to cause land to become a carbon sponge in all climates and conditions; and to jump start nature's restoration of disappearing wetlands with narrowly-focused remedial programs.

"With respect to agriculture, the plan calls for 'precision farming' that would: eliminate chemicals from agriculture by converting annual monoculture into perennial polyculture; genetically engineer crops to grow in soil irrigated by recycled, brackish or diluted salt water; create biodegradable and super absorbent materials that can be planted alongside crops to serve as mini-reservoirs keeping soil moist during droughts; and utilize sensors, drones, robots and driverless tractors to measure soil chemistry, water content, nutrients, growth and the Phytobiome: that environmental web that links crops with animals, soil, microbial communities, weather and other elements to promote growth and deter pests, perhaps using seeds coated with fungi or bacteria.

"Taking agriculture indoors, the plan would provide for immense, climate-controlled, artificial-light (LED) greenhouses to decrease the use of land, water, pesticides, antibiotics and fossil fuel, and would encourage novel farming techniques such as fertilizing crops with fish food and planting crops in fiber spun from basalt and chalk.

"The plan also contemplates building mobile desalinization plants along the coasts that can retreat from rising seas and be powered by off-shore wind farms installed over the horizon; using floodwaters to recharge underground aquifers; extracting water from the air using porous crystals; installing dual-purpose solar farms and solar panels that use the sun to not only generate a flow of electricity for the grid but to remove carbon dioxide from the atmosphere (through synthetic photosynthesis, for example); and manufacturing smaller and simpler nuclear reactors with modular technologies using modular factory fabrication to provide 'stand by' power when the sun is not shining or the wind blowing or the water flowing. To the extent possible, these efforts should attempt to capture and utilize heat in dry areas, and minimize seismic activity by building away from major fault lines.

"The plan also calls for the creation of new economic models to equitably distribute employment and income as standards of living are reduced, and to provide for graduated relief from such reductions if, as and when helpful technologies come on line. The economic models must repurpose technology away from consumption and toward reduced working hours and a wider distribution of available jobs, and perhaps provide meaningful and fulfilling free-time by subsidizing individual efforts to improve the environment or assist others in need.

"And the plan urges development of neuro-scientific methods to train basic cognitive skills targeting memory and thinking abilities in order to dampen egocentricity and enhance Cosmic Awareness.

"Finally, the plan contemplates taking action to better prepare the world's international institutions for what the future may hold.

"My time in office therefore will be dedicated to trying to reform and reposition the world's international institutions so they can more effectively deal with the severe global threats facing mankind.

"But first the question must be asked: Are humans capable of taking collective action to oppose and overcome planet-wide threats? The answer to that lies in human nature.

"Humans are essentially good. Evolution has seen to that: not because humans are special, but because that is the way evolution works. We are a loving, caring, generous, understanding, moral, forgiving and social species that has successfully passed through the sieve of evolution for more than 3.5 billion years. Those that lacked those traits are extinct. Those that retained those traits enjoyed an evolutionary advantage. Those traits will always predominate, except in a world of mass starvation and migration brought about by drought, flood, and contamination of the land and sea.

"Humans are also essentially peaceful. At any given moment, over 99 percent of the people living on the planet do so in peace and harmony raising their children, enjoying their friends, helping their neighbors, earning their living, respecting other's views and being loyal to the social structures that govern them. Those activities will always predominate, except in a world of mass starvation and migration brought about by drought, flood, and contamination of the land and sea.

"Humans also have, and probably only need, a simple moral code by which to live. It is the Golden Rule that I paraphrase as: 'Do unto others as you would have them do unto you.' Not so much because it is a guide to proper living, which it is, but because it is an excellent tool for revealing to man the horror of his own thoughts. Imagine, for example, wanting to bomb into oblivion a village in a backward country that supports terrorists killing American soldiers. Then, picture the bombs falling on your child's school, your neighbor riddled with shrapnel, your house reduced to ashes, your workplace shattered, and your fields, flowers and pets scorched. There are thousands of such examples so it behooves man to let the Golden Rule not only guide him but stay his hand when rage requires reflection.

"Turning now to the threats facing mankind, it is possible, as stated, that the combination of human overpopulation, environmental degradation and resource exhaustion will catastrophically harm life on earth, and they represent the three natural threats that require international action to overcome.

"To understand the fourth human threat we need to return to nature for guidance. Nature tells us that space-time is relative, the quantum realm is uncertain, and doubt permeates the very fabric of our existence. It is only man's conceit that convinces him he knows something without doubt. It is only rational man that knows every coin has its other side. We instinctively confirm this distinction by our natural attraction to non-judgmental people.

"The fourth threat then, the great evil currently besetting mankind, is not differences in opinion, ideology, religion, race, ethnicity, sect, or politics. It is fanaticism. It is the assertion that one's belief is not only correct but absolutely correct — an assertion in contradiction to the laws of nature; an assertion deserving of doubt if not sorrow. When that fanaticism justifies harming others, a great burden falls on mankind that requires international action to overcome.

"To counter these four planet-wide threats, I will work to reorganize the United Nations so it can more effectively act collectively should the time come when it must. It will be able to act more effectively because power will be more realistically aligned with resources, and its reformation will hopefully become the blueprint for the similar reorganization of other international institutions.

"That the reorganization might enable the United Nations to solve additional global problems would be a welcome dividend.

"That man is good, peaceful, can live by a simple moral code, and is capable of Cosmic Awareness gives me hope the reorganization can be accomplished and effective collective action can be taken as and when needed.

"The reorganization is also intended to bring relief to the United States. It can no longer bear the burden of being the world's conscience and policeman: self-appointed or in fact. It is entitled to have others share the burden. So its participation in the reorganization and indeed in all international endeavors will be proportional and it will ask no more than proportionality from others.

"The reorganization of the United Nations will involve the use of an objective test to determine whether a nation can become a permanent member of its Security Council, and that test will be a measurement of the nation's Gross Domestic Product (GDP). When any nation reaches the required level of GDP, its membership will be automatic; as will its loss of membership should it fall below that threshold. That will ensure those on the Security Council who vote for collective action have both the manpower and financial resources needed to contribute proportionally to what is approved.

"If the GDP of the United States, for example, represents 15 percent of the aggregate GDP of all those in a majority of the Security Council voting for a collective action, then it need only contribute 15 percent of the manpower and/or financial resources required, and its contribution will be conditional on the other majority voters contributing their proportional share.

"I recommend that the initial GDP level for permanent membership on the Security Council be set so that the 20 nations currently having the highest GDPs be admitted. I recommend further that no nation have a veto power over any collective action approved by the Council and that such action be determined by majority vote.

"Such a reorganized and revitalized United Nations might maintain a standing international strike force to undertake the following missions upon authorization of the Security Council: combating and defeating terrorist organizations wherever they are declared to exist; removing regimes so despotic, corrupt or chaotic their continuation is deemed inimical to world order; providing safe harbors, even in-place, for refugees until their ability to return home and rebuild their societies is enabled by conditions that allow it; and assisting in the implementation of environmental recommendations designed to benefit all species, including our own.

"Finally, the reorganization is not intended to be in derogation of the right of the United States or any other nation to act individually to protect its core interests and people. The main purpose of the reorganization is to prepare the United Nations and other international institutions for what lies ahead.

"My time in office will also be dedicated to convincing the American people that the American Revolution is on-going and a mid-course correction is necessary not only to avoid the nation becoming an empire in decline but to position it to more effectively deal with the profound threats facing it.

"Civilizations rise and fall. Ours will be no different in the fullness of time, but the refreshment of equality and idealism can postpone the decline. To be effective, that refreshment must take into account differences in American life between the time of the Founders' original intent and now. After all, no human can prescribe a form of government that will be relevant forever, much less over two hundred and twenty five years into the future.

"Has America begun its decline? That is open for debate. Certainly a gridlocked electorate, a failing educational system, a crumbling infrastructure, an erosion of the social safety net, an unemployable youth, an alarmist media, a toleration for greed, an aversion to sacrifice, an obsession with celebrity and a lessening of opportunity are grounds for concern. But they are not dispositive; especially when weighed against the amazing, hard-earned accomplishments of the American people and their extraordinary characteristics: particularly optimism, tolerance, respect for truth and love of country.

"To determine whether the United States requires a mid-course correction in its revolution, it might be helpful to surmise what the Founding Fathers would think about the state of the Union should they somehow be able to time-travel to the present day.

"I believe they would be delighted at the gridlock in Congress as proof positive that, after five thousand years of despots, tyrants, dictators, kings and emperors, they were able to fashion a government that was truly responsive to the will of its people. But I also believe they would be saddened to find the electorate so divided and gridlocked.

"I believe they would be utterly amazed at flight, genetics, nuclear energy, space exploration, advances in medicine, computers, weapons of war, cell phones, improvements in agriculture, advances in transportation, new social sciences and other extraordinary advancements since their day, and would wonder why Americans have been so timid in amending their Constitution to take the consequences of these advancements into account. The mechanism for amendment was created to be used.

"I believe they would be appalled at the transfer of the nation's wealth to a privileged few, the waning of opportunity for the many, the assault of the media on the nation's sense of well-being, the contraction of the middle class, and the unfairness and complexity of the tax system.

"I believe they would find the willingness of Americans to sacrifice for their country to have been compromised by exemptions granted the well-connected, and that such willingness can be retrieved if Americans are convinced all citizens will bear the nation's burdens equally.

"I believe they would be dismayed at their lack of foresight, in a world likely to become ever more complicated and dangerous, in failing to provide a recall mechanism by which the people could directly remove an unfit president from office.

"I believe they would realize that allowing each house of Congress to determine the Rules of its Proceedings without limitation was a mistake disrupting the checks and balances they labored to create, and that failing to use the decennial Census to prevent safe seats in the House through gerrymandering was a wasted opportunity.

"I believe they would be disappointed at the dysfunction of the Senate and the misuse of its rules to require voting supermajorities where none should exist, to prevent or postpone the very voting for which it was created, to undermine the founding principle of majority rule, and to deliver excessive power to the minority.

"I believe they would be frustrated at the ability of either house of Congress to use its rules to prevent or delay voting that might avert a fiscal emergency or to extract political contributions while Congress is in session.

"And I believe they would wonder why Americans are so supportive of majority rule at their Supreme Court but so unconcerned about it in their Congress, and how they missed the opportunity of requiring a senate supermajority to confirm Supreme Court nominees in order to ensure public support for lifetime tenure and its benefits.

"These are just a few of my suppositions regarding how the Founding Fathers would react to the current state of the Union. The conjectures of others would be just as valid.

"But be assured I am not talking of wholesale changes to our Constitution or form of government, just certain modifications to take into account modern-day realities and to fix those parts of the system that are broken.

"My time in office will therefore be dedicated to implementing a mid-course correction for the American Revolution by identifying and changing four developments in American life that represent clear and present dangers to the Union.

"What is remarkable about these four developments is that, for the most part, they are no one's fault. They simply happened as a result of the growth of the nation and the effect on it of changes in size, demographics, social values, economics, technology, war, international relations, race relations, politics, and other factors too numerous to mention. But they are harmful and should be changed by constitutional amendment or legislation, as required.

"Regarding the first clear and present danger, ask yourself what happens to the compassion, confidence, sense of security, sense of well-being and level of stress of a human being bombarded every hour of every day with news he can do nothing about of killings, thefts, fraud, double-dealing, conflicts of interest, rape, riot, slander, revenge, back-biting, cheating, rants of demagogues, foreign wars, ethnic cleansing, self-dealing, terrorism, radiation poisoning, political chicanery, mass demonstrations, lies, collapse of societies, collapse of families, failure of banks, downturn of economies, crop failures and on and on and on and on?

"And what happens when the presentation of that news too often relies on ambush, sensationalism, innuendo, rush to judgment, pandering, exaggeration, scoops above all, spin, private agendas, commercial manipulation, indifference to distress and humiliation, and appeals to the lowest common denominator?

"And what happens when delivery of that news is leveraged by an explosion of electronic communications?

"What happens is tremendous psychological damage to that human being and to all the citizens of a nation exposed to such an assault. What happens is loss of empathy, collegiality and the spirit of cooperation; loss of goodwill; loss of the willingness to share and to sacrifice; loss of optimism and confidence; and loss of a sense of well-being and security.

"What justifies the passive acceptance of this damage? Why do we bear this assault on our psychological well-being? Why do we tolerate the, 'If it bleeds, it leads' business model for news? We certainly do it to preserve and protect the freedoms of speech and press, but mainly we do it for profit. For the profit of those who own the media and who must dial up the volume of attention-getting horror each day to compete for market share in a world of ever-growing distractions.

"I submit that we are paying too high a price for this kind of expression and during my time in office I will propose that the First Amendment to the Constitution be changed, after a full and fair national debate, to prohibit those policies and practices of the media that are causing psychological damage to the people of the United States.

"Hopefully, that debate will sort out substance and relevance from trivia, speculation, superficiality and sensationalism; will determine that a 'person' for purposes of the First Amendment must be a living, breathing human being and not a fiction created by law; will authorize the regulation of campaign contributions to prevent the distortion of the democratic process by money; will explore time limits on exposure to the media and more stringent qualifications for its ownership; will consider whether making it easier for aggrieved citizens to sue the media for libel and slander can breathe life back into the right of privacy; and will examine whether courts can be reasonably empowered to restrain leaks of classified information prior to publication that are likely to harm national security — especially in an online world.

"Additionally, and hopefully, the debate will explore the best way to split-off affiliates or lines of business or percentages of business of major technology companies to ensure they do not become too big, too influential, too unmonitored, too politically powerful, too gate-keeper dominant, and too 'Big Brotherish.' The threat or use of such dismemberment should prove helpful in motivating such companies to align their business models with privacy rights and common decency.

"Finally, for those afraid of 'tampering' with the First Amendment, I submit to you that if the Founding Fathers had enough confidence Americans could distill truth from lies tolerated by the freedoms of speech and press, then they had enough confidence Americans could modify those freedoms to address changed circumstances in order to form a more perfect Union. And if that did not work, to do it again.

"Regarding the second clear and present danger, I earlier remarked that it was an open question whether America was in decline and stated that problems involving gridlock, education, infrastructure, social safety, our youth, the media, greed, sacrifice, celebrity and opportunity were grounds for concern.

"I believe almost all of these problems are caused and sustained, in whole or in part, by the massive transfer of the nation's wealth to a privileged few over the last thirty to forty years. After all, money locked up 'here' is not available 'there.' I also believe that for the most part the privileged few accomplished this transfer by working harder and being smarter than the rest of us, and by playing by the rules, so they generally deserve to keep what they have earned thus far. I also believe that their efforts were aided and abetted by the natural tendency toward monopoly in any economic system and by a political class made venal by a dysfunctional electoral system.

"I further believe that economic inequality pollutes the political system by giving the wealthy enough clout to change laws to benefit themselves; it automates bias against the poor when administrators use algorithms to determine benefit eligibility without addressing larger issues of failed policy and systemic bias; it leads to bad health and early death for the poor not only from decreased access to health care and nutrition but from chronic stress; and it ensures that where the gap between rich and poor is the greatest, environmental damage is the worst.

"This national paradigm must end or it will preclude the refreshment of equality and idealism. Going forward, the wealth of this nation must be returned to a majority of the people so the problems contributing to its possible decline can be addressed and the destabilizing threat of a shrinking middle class can be avoided.

"Therefore, during my time in office, I will recommend action to both accomplish a wholesale revision of the U.S. Tax Code in order to simplify it, and to modify those other governmental rules and regulations that facilitate inequality and promote disillusionment.

"Using a blunt force approach, I will propose that all tax credits, deductions, preferences and exemptions be eliminated in their entirety so that, after a suitable cooling off period, the debate can be about restoring them, not keeping them. That should buy time for us to sort out our priorities; to ensure preferment for ordinary citizens rather than businesses and the wealthy; and to defer restorations until their need is undeniably justified.

"On the revenue side, I will support legislation to impose higher tax brackets on the wealthy; to exact a percentage tax on the sales price of all securities transactions; to automatically share international banking and corporate data to apprehend offshore tax evaders; to impose a tax on shareholders of corporations that relocate jobs abroad or substitute contractors for employees; to impose a tax on shareholders of media or online companies that violate the provisions of a revised First Amendment; to eliminate the distinction between income and capital gains; to end all tax advantages for corporations that move intellectual property abroad or keep cash from foreign sales abroad or relocate abroad; and to impose a carbon tax on the production, distribution or use of fossil fuels based on how much carbon their combustion emits.

"I will also propose action to restrict the campaign season for federal elections to six months; to ensure federal pre-clearance of state voting laws to prevent discrimination based on race or color; to require mandatory voting for federal elections; to abolish the Electoral College in favor of direct popular vote; to set a cap on campaign contributions by institutional, special interest and individual donors; and to authorize new terms of office for, and impose term limits on, members of Congress such that House members may serve no more than two 4-year terms and Senate members may serve no more than one 8-year term, with half the Senate turning over every four years. The health and retirement benefits available to members of Congress during their time in office will be limited to participation in Medicare and a ten (10%) percent of salary, matching, retirement savings plan payable in lump sum at end of term.

"I will also propose amending the Constitution to provide that health care is a right, not a privilege, and in furtherance of that will reduce health care costs by converting the current health care system into a universal single-payer system. Then, over a 10-year period, Medicare will absorb all other health care programs by annual incremental adjustments to its age of eligibility: down from 65 and up from infancy.

"As to drugs, the single payer will be empowered to negotiate lower drug prices, permit more drugs to be imported, create more transparency in drug pricing, provide for easier drug comparisons, and implement 'value-based' pricing whereby drug prices are related to effectiveness not market conditions.

"I will also propose stronger enforcement of the nation's laws prohibiting discrimination in pay; will support indexing the national minimum wage to inflation; will recommend the conversion of all senior health and retirement programs into strictly means tested (by net worth) programs; will support the abolishment of unnecessary subsidies for business — particularly farm, fossil fuel and pharma subsidies; will recommend fixed caps on compensation, direct or indirect, for senior corporate executives based on a ratio of their compensation to the median compensation of their employees; will allow prisoners to earn early release with achievements in education; and will welcome all proposals from citizens that are reasonably calculated to return the wealth of the nation to a majority of the people.

"You might well ask: Should we take the risk that adoption of these proposals will adversely affect the economy slowing consumption and production and lowering our standard of living? If the people insist.

"You might also ask: How will the wealth of this nation be returned to a majority of the people? That, of course, is up to the elected representatives of the people but here is a plan I would support: A baseline for annual federal revenues would be established for the calendar year in which the program I recommend is adopted. Half of all future annual federal revenues above the baseline would be used to reduce the national debt and half would be allocated to the states on a per capita basis.

"Over time, if substantial reductions in the national debt occur, tax cuts can be indexed to them.

"The states may use the federal revenues allocated to them only for one or more of the following purposes: cleaning up the environment, reducing the use of fossil fuels, repairing or replacing infrastructure, strengthening the social safety net, promoting family planning and birth control, creating or preserving jobs, enhancing health and retirement programs, and advancing education: particularly the promotion of Cosmic Awareness, the teaching of best environmental practices to children, the establishment of high-quality federal colleges to serve qualified, low-income students, the re-training of workers displaced by free trade or environmental concerns, the support of research and development implementing the 10-year plan, and the reversal of superficial and unchallenging curriculums now tolerated in our middle and high schools by government and parents alike.

"The revenue will be allocated to the states, not given to them. They may select the eligible projects, contract for necessary goods or services, supervise the work, and approve the invoices, but payments will be made directly to the provider of goods or services on behalf of the states by a single-payer, with full audit powers, until a state's annual allocation is exhausted. The single-payer will be the General Services Administration and the personnel administering the program will include to the extent possible those displaced from the health care industry upon conversion to a universal single-payer system. To be effective, state contracts will need to be in compliance with then existing federal procurement requirements regarding labor standards, human rights, domestic sourcing, wages, working conditions, nondis-crimination, and the like.

"Regarding the third clear and present danger, it involves a Secret Amendment passed by Congress and the states at the time of the adoption of the Bill of Rights.

"Of course, there was no Secret Amendment but there might as well have been considering the way things have turned out. Here is how it would have read:

"'Our nation shall be governed by the rule of law which shall be applicable to all men equally. No man shall be above the law with the exception of one class of citizens who shall be allowed to pursue their own interests, however selfishly, even to the detriment of the nation. Should the government and its people be struggling to contain an economic crisis, these citizens shall be authorized to oppose and even defeat such efforts for their own personal gain. Should these citizens be found guilty of wrongdoing, no matter how many thousands or tens of thousands of people they hurt, their punishment shall be minimal and their crimes quickly forgotten. These citizens shall be authorized to spend freely to exert an influence far beyond their numbers to defeat legislation and regulation that threaten their advantages, and shall be free to rapidly invent new products and services to stay one step ahead of overworked and underpaid regulators. Finally, these citizens shall be bailed out by their countrymen if they get into financial trouble. These citizens shall be the nation's commercial and investment bankers who may be known collectively as "Wall Street."'

"Is this fantasy Secret Amendment an exaggeration? Yes, to make a point. Is it unfair to many honest, hard-working, well-intentioned members of the financial community? Yes, again to make a point. Does it fairly accurately describe Wall

Street's evolution, current privileges and influence on the economy and government? It does. Have we empowered Wall Street to ruin the economy and devastate the lives of ordinary Americans as it goes about its business? We have. Have we exacted an appropriate price for these privileges? We have not. Does Wall Street's business model represent a clear and present danger to the Union? It does.

"Since the American people obviously want a viable stock market to raise money and trade securities, it makes sense to find a new way to restrain Wall Street's excesses by raising the price it must pay for its privileges. I propose that price be greater exposure to regulation, criminal prosecution, and financial loss.

"As to regulation, I propose considerably more funding to increase the size and skill of the financial, regulatory, investigative and prosecutorial workforces so they may not only enforce regulations aggressively but research and adopt new regulations quickly. I also propose changing existing law to reinstate Glass-Steagall's separation of commercial and investment banking; to break up those commercial banks, investment banks, hedge funds, private equity funds and insurance companies deemed too big to fail by the Treasury Department; to close for five years the revolving door between Wall Street and Washington; to treat money market funds the same as commercial banks with respect to capital require-ments, reserves and fees for deposit insurance; to shut down high-speed computer-driven trading because of its inherent unfairness and potential to mindlessly destroy market value and savings; and to prohibit commercial and investment banks from owning or trading commodities because costly accidents can endanger the financial system and bid rigging and price manipulation can artificially raise consumer prices.

"As to criminal prosecution, I propose lowering the burden of proof for financial crimes from 'guilty beyond a reasonable doubt' to 'guilty by clear and convincing evidence.' I also propose the imposition of mandatory prison sentences for financial crimes far longer than those currently existing, and whistleblower rewards for exposing financial crimes far higher than those currently in place.

"As to financial loss, I propose, as indicated earlier, the imposition of a percentage tax on the sales price of all securi-ties transactions, without exception, with the possibility of refunds to suppliers of goods who must hedge to control commodities costs. I also propose a substantial increase in fines for financial fraud; fixed caps on compensation, direct or indirect, for Wall Street executives based on a ratio of their compensation to the median compensation of their employees; treatment of 'carried interest' as ordinary income if capital gains are not abolished; and higher tax rates on hedge fund and private equity income.

"Regarding the fourth clear and present danger, it involves action to fix the problems I believe the Founding Fathers would want resolved concerning recall of the president, voting for Supreme Court nominees, the relevance and rules of the Senate, the ability of either chamber of Congress to use its rules to create a fiscal emergency or extract political contributions, and the failure to use the decennial Census to prevent safe seats in the House created by gerrymandering.

"As regards the president, I propose action that will allow the people to recall the president by popular majority vote at any time for any reason. The recall will be by referendum upon petition of five percent of eligible voters in a majority of states. Petitioners may submit their signatures to the states in person or online. Upon recall, the normal procedure for succession to the office under the Presidential Succession Act of 1947, as amended, will apply.

"As regards the Supreme Court, I propose action that will require a two-thirds majority of all senators to confirm a Supreme Court nominee, and further, because their tenure will have become illegitimate retroactively, that one justice of the current Court retire on December 31st of each year for the next nine years in order of seniority.

"As regards the Senate, we once asked the states represented at the Constitutional Convention if they wanted disproportionate voting in one of the two houses of their national legislature and they said yes, and perhaps it is time to ask the other states as well and to give the original states an opportunity to reconsider. The question would be: 'Do you still want the Senate to represent lines on a map rather than people?'

"In the exercise of its disproportionate voting power, the Senate has effectively disenfranchised large segments of the population when voters in states with few citizens could thwart the will of voters in states with far more citizens, and has adopted rules granting ever more power to smaller and smaller minorities, sometimes even to a minority of one.

"Therefore, I propose action that will leave the number of a state's representatives in the Senate as is, but will provide for weighted voting that takes into account population differentials, and will prohibit the adoption of any rule that requires, directly or indirectly, voting supermajorities except as specifically set forth in the Constitution, or allows individual senators or groups of senators less than a majority to prevent or delay voting required or authorized by the Constitution. The Constitution should protect minority rights, not suffer minority abuses.

"On financial matters, I propose action that will authorize the president to declare a fiscal emergency when there is imminent danger of the government being shut down or the nation's credit being impaired, and this declaration shall require the House or Senate to vote as a body on legislation passed by the other chamber, without amendment, within three days of the declaration; provided the declaration identifies the legislation in question and certifies that it can avert the fiscal emergency. I also propose action to restrict elected federal officials from receiving political contributions while Congress is in session.

"On use of the decennial Census, I propose action that will extend the population survey used to determine a state's congressional seats to include collection of information on conservative, moderate and liberal ideological preferences, so that a nonpartisan national commission appointed by the president and confirmed by the Senate at the time of the Census can draw congressional districts for each state that ensures, to the extent possible, the total number of its representatives in the House reflects the statewide percentages of those preferences.

"That said, it is time to return to a discussion of the political experiment I ask you undertake with me. The experiment can be reversed in succeeding elections if you are displeased with the results.

"In a way the experiment is politically neutral because either a Republican President and Republican Congress, or a Democratic President and Democratic Congress can carry out the program I have been describing. But, for now, those two political parties must be jarred into sensibility by the electorate to break the gridlock in Congress caused by the electorate, and so that both parties get the message something must be done. Massively favoring one party over the other in the short term would send that message; particularly since the process can be easily reversed.

"Since I happen to be the President at this time, and since I promise to pursue the program with all my energy during my time in office, if you agree with the program I ask you to help me effectuate it by giving my party overwhelming majorities in the House and Senate in the next election. The overwhelming majority in the Senate must be sufficient to break any filibuster. If you would prefer not to vote for any particular party, simply ask any candidate running for office if he or she will support the program without qualification. If the answer is 'yes,' vote for the candidate. If the answer is 'yes, but,' vote against the candidate. If the answer is 'no,' vote against the candidate.

"I also promise to aggressively use my veto power to restrain the tendency of the party in power to misinterpret its mandate and to stray from its mission over time, and I will call out those legislators who I believe are opposing the program not from conscience but for narrow, selfish, political advantage.

"Thank you, ladies and gentlemen, for giving me the opportunity to speak to you and to work with you to recover a government of the people, by the people and for the people."

Mr. President, I hope you find this recommended speech to be helpful and I wish you the best of luck in your efforts to reform and improve America.

May I also use this opportunity to ask you to use your good offices to facilitate a scientific inquiry that, regardless of outcome, might heighten interest in science and deepen Cosmic Awareness. The inquiry will employ the scientific method that requires, among other things, the construction of a hypothesis, the testing of the hypothesis by experiment, the drawing of a conclusion from the data, and the communication of the results.

The hypothesis in this case is that time (entropy) can move in opposite directions in the same universe, and the experiment is the careful sequencing of hi-energy particle accelerator tests to spell out in simple Morse code the question, "Is anybody there?"

Let me explain: First, please note that I do not have any scientific evidence to support my hypothesis but have arrived at it by induction, inference and intuition. Therefore, the inquiry is quixotic. But the experiment to test the hypothesis is so effortless and cost-free it is worth trying. Please also note the hypothesis is based entirely on the concept of reciprocality, which is variously defined as "present or existing on both sides; each to the other; mutual," or "corresponding but reversed or inverted."

Common usage often refers to reciprocality as the yin yang or as different sides of the same coin. Yin Yang can be thought of as complimentary forces that interact to form a dynamic system in which the whole is greater than the assembled parts. Two sides of the same coin can be thought of as two things that are very closely related although they seem different.

Reciprocality pervades the universe. It is virtually impossible for man to think of a concept that does not have its other side. You need down to have up. They are both directions. You need cold to have hot. They are both temperatures. You need death to have life. They are both states of being. You need fast to have slow. They are both speeds. You need good to have evil. They are both moral judgments. These examples are but a tiny few of the inversely related, opposite reciprocals that comprise the universe.

But if the universe allows reciprocality, why can it not allow a portion of the overall universe to contain matter and energy that is separate from, and reciprocal to, the matter and energy in our portion of the universe, and is virtually undetectable because time there moves in the opposite direction of time here?

For ease of reference, I will refer to our share of the overall universe as "our universe" and the reciprocal share of the overall universe as "the reciprocal universe." I note that our universe and the reciprocal universe are present or existing on both sides, each to the other; that the reciprocal universe is corresponding but reversed or inverted; and that the reciprocal universe interacts with our universe to form a dynamic system in which the whole is greater than the assembled parts.

I also speculate that we cannot cross from our universe to the reciprocal universe without ripping the fabric of space-time. But we can communicate with each other where physics is uncertain: beyond the speed of light, through black holes, or below the size of the atom. Hence, the hi-energy particle accelerator tests.

But why time the performance of those tests to spell out in simple Morse code the question, "Is anybody there?"

If there is both our universe and a reciprocal universe, perhaps they influence each other like cable cars passing each other where the one coming down lifts the one going up and the one going up slows the one coming down. Thus, when our universe accelerates from its Big Bang, the reciprocal universe accelerates from the end of its expansion. And when our universe decelerates toward the end of its expansion, the reciprocal universe decelerates toward its Big Crunch. These effects are true for both universes and in neither case is gravity a factor. The influence of one universe on the other outweighs it and, over time, causes the flattening, structuring, distribution and uniformity of the other making inflation unnecessary.

This also raises some tricky problems. It would mean we have not yet detected the slowing of the acceleration of the expansion of our universe, and we can never detect the slowing of the deceleration of the contraction of the reciprocal universe. However, if reciprocality exists, it appears that what happens in our universe is influenced by what happens in the reciprocal universe and vice versa.

Thus, the influence of matter and energy in the reciprocal universe might be perceived as dark matter and dark energy in our universe. And the unification of general relativity and quantum mechanics might occur across the universes rather than within them, as might gravity. And the eight space-time dimensions in the combined universes might replace the ten or more suggested by string theory.

Further, the surplus of matter over antimatter in our universe might be balanced by a surplus of antimatter over matter in the reciprocal universe. And the resistance of opposing time in each universe might collapse both the quantum wave function, and gas discs needed for quasars to form, in both. And nanosecond time in our universe might be sufficiently slowed by opposing time in the reciprocal universe such that light-speed communication becomes the norm and "spooky action at a distance" becomes an illusion.

So, if our universe is almost 14 billion years old, and there is a reciprocal universe influencing our universe and everything in it, it is possible we have about 14 billion years left to get to the end of the expansion of our universe or, stating it another way, we are one-quarter of the way through our cycle of Big Bang, expansion, contraction and Big Crunch. Similarly, the reciprocal universe is three-quarters of the way through its cycle of Big Bang, expansion, contraction and Big Crunch making it about 42 billion years old.

And if the reciprocal universe is about 42 billion years old, and intelligent life there has survived its age of technology, that life would be incredibly advanced and possibly waiting for a signal from us that we are mature enough for contact. Thus, the question: "Is anybody there?"

Finally, if we do receive a reply, it would mean we have not just been building particle accelerators (for communicating below the size of the atom), and Laser Interferometer Gravitation-Wave Observatories (for communicating through black holes), and Space Telescopes like the James

Webb (for communicating with that part of the contracting reciprocal universe still beyond the speed of light), we have been building bridges.

Thank you Mr. President for your time and your consideration of my request.

Respectfully yours,

Michael J. Weinstock

The Seminar

A Play in Two Acts

By

Michael J. Weinstock

Cast of Characters

In Control Room:

Glenn Richter:	Particle Physicist, 32
Hale Broward:	Quantum Physicist, 45
Bryan Goldstein:	Computer Database Engineer, 29
Myra Carlin:	Assistant Director, High-Energy Particle Accelerator Lab, 63
Alan Branford:	High School Teacher Of The Year, 55

In Office/Conference Room:

Steven Hamcke:	Chair, Physical Sciences Department, 63
Corey Bond:	Physics Major, 22
Kamal Sood:	Astronomy Major, 22
Trish Shockley:	Biology Major, 22
Wang Chou:	Geology Major, 22
Leticia Brown:	Environmental Science Major, 22

Scene

The scenes switch back and forth between the Control Room and the Office/Conference Room.

Time

The first day of class of each month during the college year from September to May.

ACT I

Scene 1

SETTING:　We are in the Control Room of a high-energy particle accelerator lab. Mainframe computer equipment blinks and glows everywhere. Cluttered shelves, charts and open books imply ordered chaos. There is a gigantic computer screen on the rear wall, a window to its left, and a large poster of the Standard Model Of Particle Physics to its right. The poster doubles as a calendar and we can see it is the month of September. Three desks with personal computers line the wall stage right, a small conference table sits in the middle of the room, and a doorway with a nearby light switch opens stage left.

AT RISE: GLENN is at his desk looking at his computer screen. HALE is peering out the window. BRYAN is sitting at the table reading a book.

GLENN

President Putin of Russia has gone into a coma!

BRYAN

What? When?

GLENN

A few hours ago. It's on Cable News. The Russian government is urging calm. I'll bet the fight for succession is on.

HALE

Hey, guys, our guest has arrived! Myra is meeting him in the parking lot.

GLENN

Who is this guy?

HALE

A science high school teacher from Des Moines. He won this year's Best Teacher Of The Year Award and elected a tour of the lab as his prize.

(They gather around GLENN'S computer)

BRYAN

I'll bet the Russian police are going crazy.

GLENN

No, everything is quiet. People are gathering in Red Square to begin a vigil.

HALE

Anything from the U.S.?

GLENN

Just watching and waiting. The usual expressions of concern.

HALE

I don't get it. The guy was healthy as a horse. In fact, he rode one, bare-chested, to establish his macho creds.

BRYAN

(eerily)

Ask not for whom the bell tolls; it tolls for thee.

HALE

I find your sympathy to be rightfully thin.

(MYRA and ALAN enter.)

MYRA

Hi, everyone. This is Alan Branford . . . Alan, welcome to the lab.

ALAN

Nice to be here. I've looked forward to this for a long time.

MYRA

Shall we get the formal introductions out of the way. Alan, as I mentioned, I'm Myra Carlin and I'm the Assistant Director of the Voltran High-Energy Particle Accelerator Lab. This is my Control Room team: Doctor Glenn Richter, Particle Physicist; Doctor Hale Broward, Quantum Physicist; and Doctor Bryan Goldstein, Computer Database Engineer.
(They shake hands all around.)
Gentlemen, as you know Alan is here to take a tour of the facility. Alan, as you know we offer only one type of tour so some of this may seem simplistic considering your science background.

ALAN

No problem. I understand the concepts but I've always wanted to see the equipment in operation. By the way, did you hear about the President? He's in a coma.

GLENN

Putin?

ALAN

No, Trump. He's been taken to Walter Reade National Military Medical Center.

BRYAN

Seriously?

ALAN

It happened a few hours ago. Check the news.
(They rush to GLENN'S computer.)

MYRA

My, God, it's true! What the hell is going on?

HALE

(pointing at the screen)
Look! It's not just Trump and Putin. Xi of China, Assad of
Syria, and Maduro of Venezuela are in comas, too!

BRYAN

I think a robust "Oy vay!" is in order here.

ALAN

Myra, if you have to deal with this, we can reschedule . . .

MYRA

(reflecting)
No, no. I think carrying on is the best thing we can do for
now. Let's stay focused until we know more. Glenn, keep
an eye on the news. We'll show Alan around. Hale, please
bring the map of the facility up on the screen.

MYRA (Cont.)

(HALE sits down, types a command into his computer,
and a map of the lab buildings appears on the screen.
MYRA uses a laser pointer to locate the features she is
describing.)

We smash protons together in this collider and study the wreckage to reveal the structure of the subatomic world – that's the world below the size of the atom. We fire protons in opposite directions around this ten-mile ring at nearly the speed of light and guide them so they smash into each other. We use electric fields to speed and bunch up the protons, and magnets to guide them. It's all very complicated but for shorthand we simply call it "firing the protons." When we need to double check to see if the protons are actually firing, we listen to them, but on a basis hugely slowed down so we can perceive them. Hale?

(HALE types commands into his computer and we
hear five loud PINGS spaced three seconds apart.)

We place a detector where the protons collide, here. They reveal and record particles and radiation produced by the collisions and we can view them whenever we wish. Hale?

(HALE types additional commands into his computer.
The screen on the rear wall alights with static. Then,
five brilliant particle showers cascade down the screen,
four seconds apart, with static in between.)

MYRA (Cont.)

Over 160 computing centers in 40 countries analyze our data. We provide universal distribution so they can see and study the collisions on their computer screens exactly as we see them here. The calendar on the wall shows the Standard Model Of Particle Physics, which lists all the particles and forces in the universe confirmed by experiments so far.

ALAN

Can you program the computers to fire protons in specific sequences and detect specific signals?

MYRA

We can.

GLENN

(staring at his screen)

Oh, oh! It's happened again.

(They gather around his desk.)

Three more. Duterte of the Philippines, Jong-un of North Korea, and Erdogan of Turkey. All in comas.

ALAN

This is ridiculous.

BRYAN

(tremulously)
For God's sake, call 911!

MYRA

Guys, let's stick to science, shall we. There's probably a very reasonable explanation. Were they all at some international conference together?

HALE

No idea. We need more information.

ALAN

Myra, until we get more information, may I ask if the lab performs any other high-energy accelerator experiments?

MYRA

Not per se. But I did want to tell you briefly about our secondary mission. Because we have tremendous computing power here we were hired by the U.N. Intergovernmental Panel On Climate Change to look at extremely large data sets to see if we can tease out patterns, trends and associations regarding global warming. We affectionately call it the "Ass Backwards Project."

ALAN

Why is that?

MYRA

Bryan, you have the lead on this . . .

BRYAN

Normally, a person identifies a problem and then seeks a solution. Here, we use a counterintuitive approach to see if we can develop more useful information. We list various solutions and then use Big Data to try to find problems for them. If we succeed, it helps us select the best option among several solutions, or at least prevents us from going down blind alleys.

ALAN

How do you report your findings?

BRYAN

We analyze the data each month, discuss it, and submit preliminary reports to the Intergovernmental Panel throughout the duration of the project, which is nine months.

ALAN

Will there be a final report?

BRYAN

Yes, and hopefully it will answer the fundamental questions being asked by the Intergovernmental Panel.

ALAN

Which are?

BRYAN

Well, based on some very, very preliminary and unusual trends the Panel is seeing: Is the earth cooling? Is it healing itself?

ALAN

Is it?

MYRA

That, I'm afraid, is Confidential.

(BLACKOUT)

(END OF SCENE)

ACT I

Scene 2

SETTING: We are in an Office/Conference Room in the Physical Sciences Department of a major university. In the center of the room is a large conference table surrounded by five chairs. A half-podium sits on one end of the table near the the Chairman's desk, stage left. An exit door stage right joins art, bookshelves and certificates along the walls. A large calendar of astronomical wonders indicates the month is September, and a rotating blackboard is easily seen behind the table.

AT RISE: COREY, KAMAL, TRISH, WANG and LETICIA are in the room idly looking at their cell phones and laptops. STEVEN enters briskly carrying a heavy briefcase.

STEVEN

Hi, everybody! Let's get started.
> (STEVEN puts down his briefcase and stands behind the podium. They sit.)

STEVEN (Cont.)

It's nice to see you're all in your places with bright, shiny faces . . .

COREY

(singing)

. . . and this is the way to start a new day.

STEVEN

Precisely! Welcome to my experimental seminar for gifted science graduates. I am Professor Steven Hamcke, Chairman of the Physical Sciences Department, and you are here to study for your Masters. I created this little experiment to see if our discussion of certain specific topics can influence your thinking and if that thinking will show up in your theses. The small stipend I offer is to compensate you for your extra work above and beyond your regular studies. We'll meet here once a month during the school year.

KAMAL

What topics?

STEVEN

Ah, isn't that always the deep and abiding question? Shall we say topics of whimsy, topics of fate, topics of spontaneity, topics of contemplation.

LETICIA

Forgive me for saying so, Professor, but it sounds like bullshit to me.

STEVEN

(laughing)

Me too! But seriously, in my experience some of the very best ideas arise from free-flowing discussions and spontaneous declarations; even wisecracks loosen things up. We'll emphasize that, see if it makes the learning experience more relevant and focused, and, if so, expand the approach to the entire Masters program.

TRISH

But why us?

STEVEN

Best undergraduate grades; best mix of disciplines; best enrollment applications; best essays. I trust you find that sufficiently flattering? That said, why don't we get to know each other. Let's go around the table. Please state your name, where you did your undergraduate work, and your major.

COREY

Corey Bond. MIT. Physics.

KAMAL

Kamal Sood. Stanford. Astronomy.

TRISH

Trish Shockley. Duke University. Biology.

WANG

Wang Chou. University of Michigan. Geology.

LETICIA

Elvira Thunderpussy. Stankey Junior College. Quoits.

STEVEN

(laughing)

Impressive credentials! How about for real?

LETICIA

Leticia Brown. Columbia University. Environmental Science.

STEVEN

Good. Welcome. Here's how we'll proceed. We'll follow some simple rules. I'll introduce a topic and we'll discuss it at length. You can say whatever comes to mind. We hope to uncover things you know but don't know you know. Swear if you like. Walk around if it helps. WAGS are perfectly acceptable.

TRISH

What's that?

WANG

Wild ass guesses.

STEVEN

You can also ask me questions so long as they relate to science. I will not, for example, answer questions about the meaning of life.

KAMAL

How about if a tree falls in the forest, is it still the man's fault?

STEVEN

Of course, but don't tell anyone I said that. So, let's begin. Why don't we start with the topic of medicine. What in the world is happening to all the heads of state that have slipped into comas?

WANG

How many are there now?

STEVEN

50, so far. 19 in Africa, 12 in the Middle East and North Africa, eight in Asia-Pacific, seven in Eurasia, three in the

STEVEN (Cont.)

Americas, and one in Europe. All but one are considered dictators; dictators being loosely defined as heads of governments that are "not free."

COREY

So why is Trump in a coma? He's the President of a representative democracy.

STEVEN

You're right and I have no idea. I absolutely can't think of a medical reason why all of them should be in comas at the same time. There must be another explanation. Perhaps it's something they have in common. Maybe we should make a list.
(STEVEN goes to the blackboard and writes down what the students suggest.)

TRISH

Some are ruthless and power mad.
(STEVEN writes "Ruthless" and "Power Mad.")

COREY

Some are manipulative and corrupt.
(STEVEN writes "Manipulative" and "Corrupt.")

WANG

Some are killers.
>(STEVEN writes "Killers.")

KAMAL

Some are supreme egotists.
>(STEVEN writes "Egotists.")

LETICIA

Some have small peckers, were toilet trained at two weeks, and breast-fed for five years.
>(STEVEN writes "Neurotics.")

STEVEN

What about demagogues? Are any of them demagogues?

TRISH

Define "demagogue?"

STEVEN

Well, let's see. They break established rules of conduct; they use gross oversimplifications; they pretend to be of the "common people;" they inflame the passions of the mob; they urge supporters to intimidate opponents; they attack the news media; they scapegoat people of different ethnicity and religion; they fear monger; they lie; they insult and ridicule; they pin derogatory epithets on opponents; and

STEVEN (Cont.)

they behave outrageously. But hey, that's just me. Me and Wikipedia, of course.

(STEVEN writes "Demagogues.")

COREY

Not that you've given this much thought. But here's the thing. Nobody is rioting. Governments are not falling. Armies are not mobilizing. Everyone is stunned. Everyone is just watching and waiting.

KAMAL

This is so unprecedented I think people sense it is part of something bigger, something more profound. What do you think, Professor?

STEVEN

I don't think we should get ahead of ourselves. I don't think we should fantasize. Let's stick with what we know, not what we suppose. However, I do believe these heads of state have one other trait in common.

LETICIA

Which is?

STEVEN

I'm not going to tell you just yet because I'm not going to succumb to the "Stupid Statement Syndrome." You know

STEVEN (Cont.)

how you're sometimes out to dinner with friends and you're discussing politics or science or something and someone asks for your opinion and once you give it you realize you sounded stupid not just to him but to yourself as well. And that's because you weren't given an opportunity to establish a foundation: to explain the reasons for your opinion. You started at "E" without being given a chance to go from "A" to "B" to "C" to "D" to "E." Well, I'm not going to do that. I'm going to set a foundation and it's going to take time, and then I'll tell you what additional trait I believe these heads of state have in common and you can decide whether you agree with me or not. I'll see you next month.

(BLACKOUT)

(END OF SCENE)

ACT I

Scene 3

SETTING: The Control Room.

AT RISE: HALE is at his desk. BRYAN is straightening papers on the Conference Table. GLENN is changing the calendar from September to October. MYRA enters.

MYRA

Good morning.

(They all join her at the table and sit down.)

Well done on yesterday's particle experiments! We posted some really good data. Let's concentrate on climate issues today.

GLENN

You know, we've been analyzing Big Data for a month but I'm not sure in what context. What is our baseline? What assumptions do we make to begin with? In what world are we developing this information?

HALE

I agree. I think we should agree on a set of starting principles.

MYRA

Okay. Any suggestions?

GLENN

Yes. I think we should start by agreeing we live in the best of all possible worlds. We also live in the worst of all possible worlds. In other words, we are all governed by the fundamental laws of nature and they are immutable and unforgiving.

BRYAN

So there is nothing we can change?

GLENN

Correct. We can only conform. Let me give you an example. Several years ago a study was conducted in a National Park on an uninhabited island containing a large number of wolves and moose. They found that when the wolves killed too many moose, the wolves starved and nature brought predator and prey back into balance. Similarly, when there were too many moose overeating the foliage, the moose starved and nature brought predator and prey back into balance.

HALE

So wolves and moose cause climate change?

GLENN

Wiseass! No, nature always brings life back into balance so if humans outstrip the resources that support them, nature will adjust the humans.

MYRA

Okay. Assumption number one is humans better go along to get along. Any other suggestions?

BRYAN

Yes, I think we should agree that environmental degradation, overpopulation, and resource exhaustion all feed back on each other. It's a downward spiral like an aging heart which causes the liver to weaken which causes the kidneys to weaken which causes the brain to weaken and so on.

HALE

When do the balls go?

BRYAN

Rumor has it yours shriveled three years ago.

MYRA

Okay. Assumption number two: Efforts to improve the environment will be undermined by increasing population and exhaustion of resources, particularly if we turn to dirtier fuels, and efforts to slow population growth will be undermined by advances in medicine and by social pressure. Is that a fair summary?

BRYAN

It is.

HALE

What about historical baggage?

MYRA

What do you mean?

BRYAN

You know, the belief the planet is ours to exploit; the conviction our current worldview is sufficient; the instinctive reluctance to face reality; the innate desire to be led; and the primordial craving to acquire.

MYRA

What's wrong with that? It's just being human.

GLENN

I, for one, enjoy it!

BRYAN

Hey, I'm just saying. Maybe our historical baggage is preventing us from taking necessary action, and maybe it is within our power to change our historical baggage.

MYRA

Okay. Let's add a qualified third assumption. We'll assume two possibilities: one, that humans are genetically predisposed to ruin their habitat, and two, that humans can overcome this genetic predisposition by force of reason. Anything else?

HALE

I think we ought to add Russian roulette to the mix.

MYRA

Why do you say that?

HALE

What game is a person playing who lives in an earthquake zone but hopes he'll get out of danger before the earthquake hits? Or who lives near a volcano? Or who lives where hurricanes come ashore? Or who lives in a flood plain?

BRYAN

"Playing With Fire."

HALE

Yes, but I prefer Russian roulette. The question is this: Is doing nothing about global warming in the hope technology will save us at the eleventh hour a form of Russian roulette? I think it is.

MYRA

Well, okay. If no one objects, we'll add a fourth assumption that says humans will place a bet that technology will save them from global warming, and if they lose will, putting it crudely, hope to get out of Dodge by going into the ground before the shit hits the fan.

MYRA (Cont.)

(There are no objections.)
All right, are we done?

GLENN

I would like to add a prediction, not an assumption if I may.

MYRA

Will it lighten the mood?

GLENN

Probably not.

MYRA

Then, forget it! We have enough on our plate as it is.

BRYAN

I want to hear it.

HALE

Me too!

MYRA

(reluctantly)
All right, go ahead.

GLENN

It is 300,000 years from now. Historians are looking back at the evolution of life on earth and agree that the rise of

GLENN (Cont.)

homo sapiens 1.3 million years before the historians existence was the first time on earth that a species arose that not only knew something bad was happening to it and why, but had the power to do something about it, and didn't.

BRYAN

You know, you really are the fucking Prince of Darkness. Talk about perking up a guy's morale!

MYRA

Is there more?

HALE

I'd like to hear that, too.

MYRA

All right, Glenn. Please go on.

GLENN

It's still 300,000 years from now. Historians conclude the generation of man that followed ours by 100,000 years also knew what was happening to it and failed to act, as did the generation 100,000 years after that. It wasn't until the time of the historians that human enlightenment finally caught up with human technology.

MYRA

And how do we turn that into an assumption?

GLENN

We don't. It's not an assumption. It's just a wild ass guess.

MYRA

Fine. Now that we have our assumptions in hand, we can resume analyzing Big Data to see if we can spot trends, however subtle, showing the climate is cooling even as we consume, waste, pollute and degrade as never before. I can't imagine how that can happen. Anyway, let's collect another month of data before reporting our first findings.

(BLACKOUT)

(END OF SCENE)

<u>ACT I</u>

Scene 4

SETTING: The Office/Conference Room.

AT RISE: TRISH and LETICIA are chatting as are COREY and KAMAL. STEVEN enters with WANG. The students take their seats and STEVEN goes to the podium. The calendar shows October. The blackboard is blank.

STEVEN

Hello, everyone. Are you ready for a simple question?
 (They nod "yes.")
All right. What is "time"?

COREY

Time is nature's way of keeping everything from happening at once.

WANG

Time is relative. It goes fast when you're having sex and slow when you have a toothache.

KAMAL

 (to WANG)
Does time fly when you're having sex, or was it really just a minute?

84

(WANG gives KAMAL the finger.)

TRISH

Time waits for no man. Time is obviously a woman.

LETICIA

The only time a woman wishes she were a year older is when she's expecting a baby.

STEVEN

(laughing)

Yes, I'll admit there's a scintilla of humor in your comments: perhaps a jot; perhaps a tittle. But let's go to the physics expert. Corey?

COREY

The arrow of time is provided by the Second Law Of Thermodynamics, which says that in an isolated system, entropy tends to increase with time. Entropy can be thought of as a measure of microscopic disorder.

LETICIA

Say, whaaat . . . ?

COREY

(amazed she doesn't get it)

It's the one-way direction or asymmetry of time.

WANG

What the hell are you talking about?

STEVEN

(laughing again)

Perhaps I can simplify. Entropy is a fundamental law of the universe and it basically provides that everything moves from a state of order to disorder. The higher the entropy, the higher the disorder. Why this is so we don't know. It just is.

TRISH

Can you give us an example?

STEVEN

Sure. Take a standing cup of coffee. It goes from hot to lukewarm to cold. It never goes from cold to lukewarm to hot, at least not without an input of energy such as putting it in a microwave. We can count on it always becoming cold.

TRISH

Any other examples?

STEVEN

Yes. Take a newly built house that stands empty. It will go from finished to falling apart to collapsed. It will never go

STEVEN (Cont.)

from collapsed to falling apart to finished, at least not without an input of energy such as a construction crew. We can count on it always collapsing.

KAMAL

Yes, but what does that have to do with time?

STEVEN

Well, consider this.
> (STEVEN emphasizes his remarks with finger points in the air.)

Hot to lukewarm to cold. Past to present to future. Finished to falling apart to collapsed. Past to present to future. Simply stated, entropy gives us a direction we can rely on. We sometimes call that direction "time."

COREY

You know, I can grasp the passage of time on both sides of the present. I can sense it staring at a 40,000 year-old petroglyph. I can even bond with the six million year-old bones of the first hominoids and the 66 million year-old bones of the last dinosaur. But try as I might, I can't get beyond that. I cannot fathom deep time.

STEVEN

No one can. Our minds don't work that way. The best we can do is to shrink the universe into a time frame we can understand.

KAMAL

How do we do that?

STEVEN

By playing a game, of course. Let's pretend the entire 13.8 billion-year history of the universe can be compressed into one year, and that it's midnight on December 31st, and we are looking back at events that occurred during the year.

LETICIA

We can pick whatever events we want, right?

STEVEN

Certainly! But with one caveat. The event you choose must occur at an earlier date than the last one mentioned. Otherwise, we'll be bouncing around all over the place rather than transitioning smoothly back in time. I'll start. Columbus one second ago!

TRISH

The first anatomically modern human six minutes ago!

WANG

An ape at 10:15 this morning!

TRISH

A bird on December 27th!

LETICIA

A mammal on December 25th!

WANG

A dinosaur on December 24th!

TRISH

An insect on December 21st!

LETICIA

A fish on December 20th!

WANG

A land plant on December 18th!

COREY

A multi-cellular organism in November!

KAMAL

A single-celled organism in September!

COREY

Our solar system in August!

KAMAL

The Milky Way in March!

COREY

The Big Bang on January 1st!

STEVEN

Way to go, team!

TRISH

That was fun. You got any other games?

STEVEN

"Bingo" and "Trivial Pursuit."

TRISH

Ask a stupid question . . . Well, at least those games are within our collective IQ.

STEVEN

I do have a couple of additional questions, however, which I would ask you to consider for discussion at future meetings.
(STEVEN goes to the blackboard.)
We discussed time, entropy if you will, having a direction. But can it have more than one direction? When I was young, I would think about time and how it moved from the beginning of the universe to the end of the universe . . .

STEVEN (Cont.)

(STEVEN makes two dots on the blackboard and connects them with a long, horizontal arrow.)

. . . and wondered if it were possible for time to move perpendicular to that direction . . .

(STEVEN bisects the first arrow with a second, downward arrow.)

. . . so that every moment is both the beginning and end of the universe.

COREY

What did you conclude?

STEVEN

It was nonsense. But Einstein proved time was flexible and didn't have to flow at a steady rate but could speed up and slow down depending on the circumstances. That established the concept that time could "be" more and "do" more than we think. That being the case, I ask you to consider if time can move in opposite directions in the same universe?

(STEVEN erases the two arrows and draws two more, one under the other, pointing in opposite directions.)

WANG

You said you had a second question for us?

STEVEN

Yes. How does the passage of deep time connect to the common trait we seek for the heads of state who are still in comas?

(BLACKOUT)

(END OF SCENE)

ACT I

Scene 5

SETTING: The Control Room.

AT RISE: The team is testing the equipment. BRYAN and HALE are at their computers. MYRA and GLENN watch the screen from opposite sides of the room. We hear the five PINGS, just as before, and then see the five particle showers, just as before. The calendar shows November.

MYRA

Good test! Good test!

(MYRA goes to the table and is joined there by HALE and GLENN. BRYAN remains at his computer.)

Guys, I have to ask you. Please, please, no more rubber ducks. The Custodial Department is driving me crazy. Okay?

(They say nothing but look around the room in perfect innocence.)

Fine. Today we're going to decide what interim findings we want to present to the Intergovernmental Panel based on our examination of Big Data over the last two months. We will structure our discussion in strict accordance with the rules and regulations of the Ass Backwards Project. This means you must first present the solution, then find a

MYRA (Cont.)

problem for it, then identify trends relating to it. Bryan will put your visuals on the screen.

GLENN

You realize, don't you that this study is going to provide a very informative secondary benefit. When all is said and done, we're going to identify for anyone interested the difference between where we are and where we need to be with respect to fighting climate change. People may not be too happy with the results.

MYRA

Be that as it may, the chips fall where they may. Hale, why don't you begin?

HALE

First, the solution: We need to plant or replant millions of trees in new or missing forests. Second, the problem: The earth's carbon sinks are starting to fail.

MYRA

Which ones?

HALE

All of them. Plants, forests, soil, the tundra, the ocean: the sinks that have been removing carbon dioxide from the atmosphere for millions of years. CO_2 is one of the most

HALE (Cont.)

powerful greenhouse gases warming the planet. Now, the sinks are releasing tons of it back into the atmosphere.

BRYAN

(from his desk)

It's true. Warming land, warming seas, forest fires, blight, even melting permafrost. They all contribute to the release.

GLENN

Surely you don't believe planting trees is going to stop all that?

HALE

No, it's just one of many things we can do that could help. Let me show you where we stand on the screen.

(BRYAN enters commands into his computer. The screen lights up with a map of the world.)

Here is an estimate of what the world's forest cover looked like five hundred years ago.

(Large red circles appear in various countries known to be heavily forested.)

Here is what it looks like today without tree planting.

(The red circles shrink considerably.)

Here is what it looks like with the tree planting reported by various governments so far.

(The red circles expand slightly.)

HALE (Cont.)

And here's what it looks like from satellites yesterday.
(The red circles expand substantially.)

MYRA

Wait a minute! You're saying the satellites show more forest cover than we think exists?

HALE

That's right.

MYRA

By how much?

HALE

Fifteen percent. I believe that is the kind of trend the Intergovernmental Panel is looking for.

MYRA

But what caused that?

HALE

Hey, I jus' reports 'em, I don' splains 'em.
(Silence.)

BRYAN

He's not alone. I looked at the status of permanent ice all over the globe: the ice sheets on Greenland and Antarctica; the glaciers in the mountains.

MYRA

The solution?

BRYAN

The solution is we have to cause ice sheets and glaciers to grow or stabilize. The problem is that if they melt, sea levels will rise around the globe.

GLENN

He's right. As seawater reaches further inland it will have devastating effects on coastal habitats. It will cause aquifer and agricultural soil contamination, destructive erosion, lost habitat for fish birds and plants, and wetland flooding.

BRYAN

Not to mention burying coastal cities in possibly 260 feet of water.

GLENN

All very neat, but why would you suggest a solution we can't possibly implement?

BRYAN

It's not the solution that interests me, it's the trend. Let me show you.

    (BRYAN types a command into his computer. The screen again lights up with a map of the world.)

BRYAN (Cont.)

Here is an estimate of what the world's ice cover looked like one hundred years ago.

(Large blue circles appear in locations known to have permanent ice sheets or glaciers.)

Here's what it looked like three years ago.

(The blue circles shrink dramatically.)

And here's what the satellites show it looked like a few days ago.

(The blue circles expand by a clearly visible amount.)

That's an eighteen percent increase.

HALE

Jesus Christ!

BRYAN

Jesus Christ, indeed.

MYRA

Well, the satellites seem to be the key to spotting trends that make no sense. What else are they showing?

GLENN

The solution: We have to slow the uptake by the world's oceans of carbon dioxide from the atmosphere. The problem I identify is that the uptake is causing ocean acidification

GLENN (Cont.)

that is killing the coral, and the loss of coral means loss of habitat for the world's fish.

BRYAN

You just did the same thing you accused me of doing! You're suggesting a solution we can't possibly implement.

GLENN

Not entirely true. An estimated 30 to 40 percent of the carbon dioxide from human activity released into the atmosphere dissolves into oceans, rivers and lakes. Perhaps we can do something about that.

MYRA

But what is the trend you spotted?

GLENN

I'll show you. Bryan?
    (BRYAN types a command into his computer. The screen again lights up with a map of the world.)
Here is an estimate of the largest coral reefs in the world's oceans from 100 years ago. It includes the Great Barrier Reef and the massive reef off of Belize.
    (Large green circles appear on locations known to have large coral reefs.)

GLENN (Cont.)

Here is what the satellites show the reefs looked like five years ago.

(The green circles shrink dramatically.)
Here's what they looked like a week ago.

(The green circles grow by a clearly visible amount.)
That's an eleven percent increase.

HALE

This is nuts. I'm wondering if we should even report these findings.

MYRA

We really have no choice. But as I sit here and listen, the thought of all the innocent species we have placed in harm's way breaks my heart. What are we, a planetary virus?

BRYAN

As I listen I wonder how we got into this mess.

GLENN

I think it started at the beginning of the Industrial Revolution when man declared war on the discomforts and inconveniences of nature. Had we been able to hear Nature speak at that time, we would have heard, "You're kidding, right?"

(BLACKOUT)

(END OF SCENE)

<u>ACT I</u>

Scene 6

SETTING: The Office/Conference Room.

AT RISE: This time it is TRISH who is late. The students are chatting amiably. LETICIA is eating a hot dog. The Professor writes at his desk. TRISH enters and they take their positions at the conference table. The calendar shows November. The blackboard is empty.

TRISH

Sorry I'm late.

STEVEN

No problem. How is everyone today?

LETICIA

Corey is becoming one with the universe, Wang is learning to center his "Wa," and I'm practicing deep throat on a hot dog.

STEVEN

(laughing)

Wonderful! It's always heartwarming for a teacher to find his students operating well within their capabilities. I am pleased to announce that today is "Astounding Facts About

STEVEN (Cont.)

The Universe Day." We are going to explore the universe from the phenomenally large to the unimaginably small at hyper speed.

KAMAL

Why hyper speed?

STEVEN

Spontaneous declarations please me. So, unless anyone has an objection, which will, of course, be ignored, let's begin.
(STEVEN goes to the blackboard.)
How did the universe begin?

COREY

A quantum emergence.
(STEVEN writes "Quantum Emergence" on the blackboard.)

KAMAL

A multiverse.
(STEVEN writes "Multiverse" on the blackboard.)

WANG

A Big Crunch.
(STEVEN writes "Big Crunch" on the blackboard."

STEVEN

Anyone else? No? Well, I would add "some other agency" since this is all speculative.

(STEVEN writes "Some Other Agency" on the blackboard.)

Please explain your responses.

COREY

A quantum emergence, simply stated, is the emergence of the universe out of nowhere. Stating it less simply, it is the emergence of space-time in quantum gravity.

KAMAL

A multiverse is a hypothetical group of multiple separate universes including the one in which we live.

WANG

A Big Crunch is how the universe might end because the expansion of space stops and then reverses into collapse. The question is: Does the collapse cause a new Big Bang resulting in a never-ending cycle of universes?

COREY

All of which implies there is no need for God.

TRISH

No! God could have created any of the universes!

STEVEN

I don't know about that, but I do believe people of faith can find God here if they wish . . .

(STEVEN draws a circle around "Some Other Agency.") Anyway, let's begin. We'll go from the very large to the very small. Call out anything that comes to mind. Joke if you want to. Give some thought to what this has to do with the leaders in comas.

COREY

The visible universe is 13.8 billion years old and contains about 200 billion galaxies. I say "visible" because there may be billions of galaxies farther out that we cannot see because they are moving away from us faster than their light can reach us. Thus, the universe could be 250 times or more larger than it is.

KAMAL

The Milky Way is ten billion years old, is 100,000 light years across, and contains 200 billion stars. The sun goes around it once every 230 million years and is in its 20th orbit since the Milky Way was formed.

WANG

The Milky Way is mostly empty space. If you squeezed all the empty space out of it, you would have a cube of stars that fits inside the orbit of Neptune.

COREY

The speed of light limits how fast cause and effect can occur.

LETICIA

This discussion is the cause. My full bladder is the effect.

STEVEN

(laughing)
Go if you need to go.

LETICIA

Just kidding. Stars drift. What was once near us could now be millions if not billions of miles away.

KAMAL

There are 10,000 stars within 100 light years of us. At the maximum speed we can travel, it would take 40,000 years to reach the nearest star. How many generations is that?

TRISH

Could someone remind me what a light year is, and is it faster than Speedy Gonzales?

COREY

The speed of light in a vacuum is the top speed in the universe. How far light travels in one year is called a light year. It travels at 186,000 miles per second. A Gonzales light year is faster.

WANG

The earth is known as a rocky planet. It rotates at about 1,000 miles an hour and has a diameter of 7,926 miles. It has a solid iron-nickel core, surrounded by a liquid metal outer core, surrounded by a mostly solid mantle, surrounded by a crust three to 120 miles thick.

LETICIA

Sounds like a pizza.

KAMAL

Here's something I find really interesting. It is thought life cannot exist without water. Where water can exist is called the habitable zone, which is not too hot and not too cold. Most of the exoplanets we've discovered have orbits smaller than Mercury's, which would likely be outside the habitable zone. Our solar system with its inner rocky planets and its outer gas giants is definitely not typical.

TRISH

This is what you find interesting?

WANG

"I" certainly do! In fact you'll be delighted to learn the earth has 20 major tectonic plates and seven of them support continents. They slide around on top of the upper mantle

WANG (Cont.)

in response to movements in the mantle, which moves in response to heat rising from below.

TRISH

Be still my beating heart.

LETICIA

The length of the entire DNA in the human body is 193,000 times the distance from the earth to the moon.

KAMAL

Matter in the human body is one hundred million trillion times more concentrated than matter in interstellar space.

LETICIA

The number of all the humans who ever lived is 110 billion.

COREY

Now I understand why we get the senior discount.

TRISH

Agriculture covers about 15 percent of the earth's land surface and involves one-third of the human population. There are only about 200 plant and 30 animal species involved in agriculture.

COREY

The atom is so small that if your fist were the size of the nucleus, the entire atom would extend to about five kilometers in all directions.

KAMAL

Some experiments suggest that an electron is at least ten million times smaller than the nucleus.

WANG

Planck scale is the smallest meaningful distance in physics. At this scale there is no longer any possiblity of making genuine measurements.

COREY

In powers of ten, humans exist almost halfway between the inconceivably big and the unimaginably small.

STEVEN

Ladies and gentlemen that was very well done! Very well done! Now, it's my turn and I would like to offer this quote from a book entitled "The Zoomable Universe" written by Caleb Sharf and illustrated by Ron Miller. The quote says, "Whatever we do to the Earth, and whatever we do to life here, the planet will carry on and life will keep unfolding, relegating our era to a thin band in some future sedimentary rock." I think that sentiment is justified by the scale of the

STEVEN (Cont.)

things we've been discussing here, and could prove most useful in framing future thought. I'll see you next month and will give you my opinion on the additional common trait shared by the heads of state currently in comas.

(BLACKOUT)

(END OF SCENE)

<u>ACT I</u>

Scene 7

SETTING: The Control Room.

AT RISE: MYRA, GLENN, and BRYAN are at the table engaged in heated conversation. The calendar shows December.

GLENN

. . . but it's a very useful approach! It's worked well so far.

MYRA

That may be but the Intergovernmental Panel is paying the bills and they want us to take a less oblique, more direct approach. They think the way we're going about it is a bit unscientific and a little frivolous.

    (HALE enters.)

GLENN

That's bullshit!

MYRA

That may be but the last thing we need is to look unscientific and frivolous.

HALE

What's going on?

GLENN

The Intergovernmental Panel wants us to stop using the Ass Backwards method and simply identify problems, offer solutions, and reveal trends.

HALE

But that's exactly what we've been doing, only backwards!

MYRA

Yes, but we had to use satellite data to do it. There are too many other problems that are not susceptible to assessment from overhead. Look, they were thrilled with what we did and very grateful, but they want us to refine our approach to better tease out ground-hidden trends.

BRYAN

That's too bad because I've discovered a hell of a trend! I did, however, have to use satellites to do it.

MYRA

What do you mean?

BRYAN

Here's the solution: We need to stop building out and only build up or over. You want to build something, fine, but build it over or build it higher. Don't use new land for it.

HALE

And the problem?

BRYAN

Developed land can't breathe. It's covered with concrete. It can't grow anything that takes up carbon dioxide and releases oxygen. It can't absorb rain so its runoff causes flooding and contaminates rivers and seas. It blights the land and steals beauty from nature.

GLENN

So where do we put all the people?

BRYAN

We fix up where they live. We put them higher.

MYRA

And the trend?

BRYAN

I'll show you.

> (BRYAN goes to his desk and types a command into his computer. The screen lights up with a map of the world.)

Here is an estimate of all the large cities and towns around the world 100 years ago.

BRYAN (Cont.)

(Large orange circles appear on the screen where large cities and towns were thought to have been.)

Here are the large cities and towns around the world two years ago.

(The orange circles enlarge dramatically and even cover new territory.)

And here are the same large cities and towns the satellites imaged one week ago.

(The orange circles shrink by a clearly visible amount.)

That's a nine percent decrease.

MYRA

Shit! I hate phenomenon without explanation. (Beat) Okay, we'll report it, Thanks, Bryan.

(MYRA sighs.)

I guess it's time to put the Ass Backwards method to bed and bring back the old tried and true "problem, solution, trend." So, let's talk about mass starvation and mass migration. What does the Big Data show?

GLENN

(reading his notes)

The current world population of 7.3 billion is expected to reach 8.5 billion in 2030, 9.7 billion in 2050, and 11.2

GLENN (Cont.)

billion in 2100 – with everyone trying to keep cool in summer and warm in winter.

HALE

(reading his notes, as well)

There are some studies that say ten billion people are the uppermost population limit where food in concerned. Other studies say the maximum carrying capacity of the earth based on food resources will probably fall short of ten billion because too few people will agree to stop eating meat.

MYRA

You know, I've been looking at this as well. The consequences of overpopulation are grim. Exhaustion of natural resources will occur sooner. Deforestation, desertification, extinction of animal and plant species, and adverse changes in the water cycle will accelerate.

BRYAN

I don't think I can add much happy news. It's pretty well agreed that mass starvation will cause mass migration which will, in turn, lower living standards worldwide, overcrowd cities, increase social conflict, and possibly make war more likely.

MYRA

All right, enough! I think we understand the problem. How do we feed all these people?

GLENN

The days of dropping seeds into the ground and hoping for the best are over. We need to implement precision farming.

MYRA

Which involves?

HALE

Eliminating chemicals from agriculture by converting annual monoculture into perennial polyculture.

GLENN

Perhaps engineering crops to grow in soil irrigated by recycled, brackish or salt water.

BRYAN

Maybe creating biodegradable and super absorbent materials that can be planted alongside crops to serve as mini-reservoirs keeping soil moist during droughts.

HALE

Possibly using sensors, drones, robots and driverless tractors to measure soil chemistry, water content, nutrients, growth and the phytobiome.

MYRA

The phytobiome?

HALE

That's the environmental web that links crops with animals, soil, microbial communities, weather and other elements to promote growth and deter pests, perhaps using seeds coated with fungi or bacteria.

MYRA

But what about extreme weather? It could still disrupt agriculture. What do we do about that?

BRYAN

Let me show you.

(BRYAN types some more commands into his computer and the screen lights up with a photo of huge greenhouses in The Netherlands stretching mile after mile into the distance.)

We take agriculture indoors by building immense, climate controlled, artificial LED-light, multi-story, greenhouses.

MYRA

Which do what?

BRYAN

They decrease the use of land, water, pesticides, antibiotics, and fossil fuels, and encourage novel farming techniques

BRYAN (Cont.)

such as fertilizing crops with fish food and planting crops in fiber spun from basalt and chalk.

MYRA

It's impressive. But do you see any trends here?

HALE

Yes, but only with respect to population growth, not agriculture where progress is being made. Recent combined demographic and medical studies are showing that infertility rates are rising around the world.

MYRA

Now, there's a perfect solution! Hard to credit though. We'll definitely tell the Intergovernmental Panel about it. Meanwhile, I'm late for a going away party.

(She gathers her things and leaves.)

HALE

This has depressed the hell out of me and I know of only one way to get out of it. What do you think?

(They all freeze, look at each other with stupid grins, edge toward their desks, and nod in agreement.)

I DECLARE DUCK HUNTING SEASON TO BE OFFICIALLY OPEN!!

(They run to their desks, pull out boxes full of yellow rubber ducks, and chase each other around the room throwing ducks at each other as hard and as fast as they can until the room is littered with ducks, they collapse in exhausted laughter, and GLENN wears a box upside-down on his head.)

(BLACKOUT)

(END OF SCENE)

ACT I

Scene 8

SETTING: The Office/Conference Room.

AT RISE: STEVEN and COREY are writing equations on the blackboard. TRISH and LETICIA are comparing notes. KAMAL reads. WANG enters and they all take their positions at the table. The calendar shows December.

STEVEN

Who wants fame and fortune?

ALL

Me!

STEVEN

Which one?

COREY

First, fame and fortune. Then, fortune and fame.

STEVEN

What would you do with the money?

KAMAL

Never fly coach from India.

TRISH

Make every effort to live rich rather than die rich.

WANG

Spend half of it on partying, booze and women and squander the rest.

COREY

One Porsche, one Lamborghini, and three Ferraris.

LETICA

(speaking breathlessly and batting her eyes)
I would work for world peace and love and understanding for all.

STEVEN

I see. Have you ever asked yourself why you need to acquire more and more stuff? After all, all you really need is food, water and shelter. Anything above that is excess. Anything above that is wretched excess.

KAMAL

Because the guy who dies with the most toys, wins.

STEVEN

Yes, I've heard that. Money is nice. But this is a science seminar and I'd like to know where this compulsion to acquire comes from.

TRISH

We tend to equate buying things with positive emotions and learn to believe buying new things will make us happy.

STEVEN

But what is the physical cause for that?

TRISH

When we see a product we like, an area of the brain lights up called the "nucleus accumbens." This triggers the brain's pleasure center and it makes the brain feel good by showering it with dopamine.

LETICIA

That's rather clinical. It's easier to say that just thinking about an acquisition brings happiness to materialistic people.

STEVEN

But the urge to acquire goes even deeper than that, doesn't it?

WANG

Actually, yes. The impulse to buy and possess things relates to Darwin's theory of evolution – to the survival of the fittest. Since natural resources are scarce, humans compete over them and try to claim as much as possible.

STEVEN

Do you think that gets baked into the genes, over time?

WANG

I do.

STEVEN

What else might get baked into the genes? How about lions attacking the campsite at night?

TRISH

Same thing. Today, our materialism is a product of our restlessness and constant wanting. But our restlessness and constant wanting started out as evolutionary mechanisms designed to keep us alert and safe from predators.

LETICIA

It's odd isn't it that, originally, our dissatisfaction kept us on the lookout for ways of improving our chances of survival. Now, it just makes us want to shop.

STEVEN

Here's what fascinates me. If someone knew all this, the evolutionary and biological history and the pleasure mechanisms in the brain, would he still be materialistic? Would he still want to acquire and possess well beyond his needs?

COREY

I don't think so, but I'd want to check with my Ferrari dealer first.

STEVEN

Right. But what about this: Is there a duty on the part of someone who rises higher and higher in society to moderate his or her cravings so they don't hurt other people?

(They think on it but no one answers.)
Okay, That pretty much covers the subject of "fortune." What about "fame?" Where does the biological necessity for fame come from?

TRISH

One theory says it has its roots in the experience of neglect, in injury. Unless someone in the past made you feel extremely insignificant, you would not need, want or seek fame.

STEVEN

Surely it goes deeper than that?

WANG

Yes. Humans are social animals who have a deep psychological need to be approved and liked by others: a need as strong as food, water or shelter.

STEVEN

And the source of this need?

LETICIA

It's pretty simple. It's a lot safer to be with the clan in the village than out on the plain by yourself. Friends kill enemies; friends supply food; friends become lovers; friends ensure survival.

STEVEN

Knowing that, does one have a duty to curb one's narcissism as one rises higher in society if it hurts other people?

COREY

Ah, I get it! This has something to do with the leaders who are in comas.

STEVEN

That's right. So, please let me tell you what I believe is the additional trait they all have in common. But first let me say I'm grateful to you for having given me the time to lay a foundation for my opinion. The trait they all have in common is that they're clueless. They are oblivious to the wider world around them. In the face of all this . . .

(STEVEN sweeps his arm as though taking in the entire world.)

. . . in the face of the Big Bang, galaxies and stars; in the face of deep time, entropy and the arrow of time; in the face of evolution, DNA and all the people who ever lived; in the

STEVEN (Cont.)

face of molecules, atoms and particles; and in the face of the known origins of fame and fortune; in the face of all this, these people think they're important.

(STEVEN let's it sink in and goes to the blackboard)) And because they think they're important, they think they're entitled. And because they think they're entitled, we get this . . .

(STEVEN flips the blackboard over and we see that the words "Ruthless," "Power Mad," "Manipulative," "Corrupt," "Killers," "Egotists," "Neurotics" and "Demagogues" are still on it.)

But if they were aware, if they had vision, they would be humble, and if they were humble, perhaps love, compassion and understanding would prevail.

LETICIA

So, you believe the meek should inherit the earth?

STEVEN

No, I believe it is absolutely essential that the meek inherit the earth.

WANG

But how can you be sure these leaders, even if imbued with a wider vision, would act any differently?

STEVEN

I can't, obviously. But I think it is very important for all humans to climb down from their high horse of self-importance and embrace humility if they want to avoid the more disastrous consequences of global warming, overpopulation and resource exhaustion. We'll discuss it next semester. But for next month, I want to discuss Faust.

(BLACKOUT)

(END OF SCENE)

ACT I

Scene 9

SETTING: The Control Room.

AT RISE: MYRA, GLENN, and BRYAN are gathered around the conference table examining blueprints and computer printouts. Behind them particle showers cascade down the screen, just as before, and will continue to do so for a while. The calendar shows January. HALE enters.

HALE

(noticing the screen)

What's going on?

MYRA

We received a request from physicists at the University of California in Irvine to rebroadcast particle showers we saw on October 16th between 10:05 and 13 seconds, and 10:28 and 31 seconds, a.m. They think they spotted something interesting and would like the particle community to review and comment. The screen should go off in a little while.

HALE

Are those blueprints?

GLENN

Yes. They're blueprints for ten of the largest desalination plants in the world.

HALE

Why are we looking at them?

MYRA

It's part of our project for the Intergovernmental Panel. I asked Glenn to research it.

(They sit.)

HALE

Why do we care how they're constructed? What's important is what they do.

GLENN

Not entirely. Let me give you some background. The problem we face, of course, is that the world is running out of fresh water.

HALE

Tell me about it. I've had to cut back on showers twice this week because of the drought.

BRYAN

I thought you smelled a bit ripe.

GLENN

Here are the statistics: Seventy percent of the Earth's surface is water. Of that, 97.5 percent is seawater unfit for human consumption. The freshwater we do have is under severe stress because of the rise in populations and temperatures.

HALE

What do you mean by "severe stress?"

GLENN

In 2000, global water demand was projected to increase by 55 percent by 2050. Seventy percent of all global freshwater is used for agriculture, and that amount will need to grow by some 69 percent by 2035 to feed growing populations.

HALE

No problem. The glaciers are expanding. Right?

GLENN

Yes, problem. The glaciers appear to be growing but we can't be sure of that or if it will continue. The bottom line is many of the world's freshwater sources are being drained faster than they can be replenished. Of the world's major aquifers, 21 out of 37 are receding.

HALE

So you want to build desalinization plants to replace the fresh water?

GLENN

Yes, but there's a problem. After the fresh water they create is extracted, the water that is left over is super saturated with salt and harms the environment when put back into the ocean. Also, they use tremendous amounts of electricity from the grid to operate and this increases greenhouse gases.

HALE

So, no solution.

GLENN

Well, possibly. The Intergovernmental Panel received a recommendation that thousands of mobile desalinization plants be built on coasts around the world, which would be powered by offshore wind farms installed over the horizon. They would be mobile to retreat from rising seas. With enough clean power, surplus freshwater could be produced to dilute the salt water before it goes back into the ocean.

HALE

That's a good idea! Who came up with that?

GLENN

No one knows. The recommendation was submitted anonymously.

(The screen goes dark. They don't notice.)

MYRA

Glenn, did any other solutions present themselves?

GLENN

A couple that were interesting. One was to build sluices, dikes, pipelines and aqueducts locally to recharge underground aquifers with floodwaters. Expanding on that, wouldn't it be great if we could use pumps, pipelines and aqueducts in the U.S. to draw off floodwaters in the east to fill reservoirs in the west.

MYRA

What was the other solution?

GLENN

It turns out you can extract water from the air using porous crystals. The trick is to capture water vapor in the air in arid regions and convert it to running water for human use. But I don't think anyone knows how many crystals it would take.

MYRA

Did you look for trends?

GLENN

Trust me, I was looking for trends all along, but nothing jumped out at me. There were, however, a couple of interesting

GLENN (Cont.)

coincidences. Branton Energy has gone bankrupt. It is the largest owner of crude oil, liquid and natural gas pipelines in the world. Its assets are available to the highest bidder.

BRYAN

Which will probably be another oil company.

GLENN

Maybe. You never know.

MYRA

What about the other coincidence?

GLENN

I don't think it's a big deal but when I looked up porous crystals at the Patent Office, I found that a new patent had been issued for manufacturing them in bulk.

MYRA

Well, we can't report coincidences as trends. Let's keep those to ourselves. Bryan, did the Department Of Energy send you the reports you requested?

BRYAN

They did. I'm drowning in them and let me tell you it's a new world. In the past, our biggest concern was how to

BRYAN (Cont.)

keep the electricity flowing and the lights on. Now, it's how to keep the electricity flowing and the lights on without burning fossil fuels when the wind isn't blowing or the sun isn't shining or the water isn't flowing.

GLENN

You're referring to renewables, right? Wind farms, solar panels and dams?

BRYAN

Yes. About 25 percent of global electricity now comes from renewables and they're growing rapidly, thankfully.

MYRA

So how do you keep the electricity flowing and the lights on? How do you provide "stand by" power?

BRYAN

Nuclear energy. But not by building huge nuclear power plants but by manufacturing smaller and simpler nuclear reactors with modular technologies using modular factory fabrication for more local use.

HALE

It will never fly. People don't want to risk nuclear fallout in their back yards.

BRYAN

Okay, they can suffer.

MYRA

I've heard solar panels can do double duty. Is it true?

BRYAN

Maybe. They're hoping to install dual-purpose solar farms and solar panels that use the sun to not only generate electricity for the grid but to remove carbon dioxide from the atmosphere, perhaps through synthetic photosynthesis. It's still being developed.

MYRA

So what trends do you see?

BYRAN

The accelerating growth of renewables is the trend. Why they're growing faster than expected is the question.

MYRA

Okay, for the next reporting cycle, I want to look at endangered fisheries, sustainability in cities, and new economic models for distributing employment equitably.

HALE

(sarcastically)

Is that all?

MYRA

No. I also want to talk about what the hell is causing these favorable trends and coincidences. Who or what is helping us?

(BLACKOUT)

(END OF SCENE)

ACT I

Scene 10

SETTING: The Office/Conference Room.

AT RISE: The students and the Professor are at their positions at the conference table. The blackboard still has the words "Ruthless," "Power Mad," "Manipulative," "Corrupt," "Killers," "Egotists," "Neurotics" and "Demagogues" on it. The calendar shows January.

STEVEN

. . . which presents three huge problems for universities: funding, diversity and faculty parking.
   (They laugh.)
All right, I still want to explore fame and fortune but this time through the eyes of literature.

TRISH

And this has what to do with science?

STEVEN

You'll find out. But first, who was Faust?

KAMAL

Wasn't he the guy who sold his Honda to the Devil?

COREY

No, that was Hidalgo Schwartz who teaches Atheism at Yale.

STEVEN

Let me quote:

(STEVEN reads from his notes.)

"Faust was a cultured intellectual who, though very prosperous, was quite dissatisfied with his life, so he made a pact with the Devil for unlimited knowledge and worldly pleasures in exchange for his soul."

LETICIA

Looks like he needed to make his deal more artful.

WANG

Not if he planned to screw the Devil in the end.

STEVEN

I should think that would be hard to do. You should know that the phrase to "strike a Faustian bargain" is derived from the fable and describes a person who is willing to sacrifice anything to slake an unlimited thirst for power and knowledge.

LETICIA

Sounds like my sister.

STEVEN

Who else in literature made a pact with the Devil?

COREY

Homer Simpson sold his soul to the Devil in exchange for a donut.

TRISH

God made a pact with the Devil. They bet over Job's soul.

STEVEN

Okay. But if you wanted to sell your soul to the Devil, how would you go about it?

WANG

Depends who you want to do business with. You could dial-a-demon, hire an attorney who specializes in demonic contract law, or consult with people who have already contracted with the Devil, like proctologists.

STEVEN

What if you wanted to get out of a deal with the Devil? How would you go about it?

LETICIA

Learn to play the fiddle and outplay him. Also, you can hire an exorcist at "Exorcists.org" and pay by credit card.

STEVEN

What if you discovered a really important secret about existence that the Devil wasn't ready to disclose and he came to you wanting to make a deal. What would you ask for?

COREY

A Porsche, a Lamborghini, and three Ferraris.

TRISH

I'd ask him to hide Corey's car keys.

WANG

My requests would be modest. Good health, Good friends. A lot of money, A mansion. Second homes in St. Moritz, Bora Bora and Carmel. A flat in London. A private railcar. A private jet. A private helicopter. A gigantic yacht. And a huge penis.

LETICIA

You should run for President.

STEVEN

Would you ask the Devil "not" to make you rich and famous?

KAMAL

Why would I do that?

STEVEN

Maybe the secret you discovered was so profound it made the idea of fame and fortune ludicrous, almost embarrassing.
(They think on it.)
Anyway, let's talk about deals with God. Except I'm going to refer to a "Higher Power" from now on rather than God to cover all the deities. So, who in literature made deals with a Higher Power?

TRISH

The Bible says Moses did to spare the Israelites at Mt. Sinai, and Abraham did to save the righteous people of Sodom and Gomorrah from destruction.

COREY

Frankenstein did with his maker, Dr. Victor Frankenstein.

WANG

Samson did when he agreed to never cut his hair.

TRISH

Noah did when he was promised life would never again be destroyed by the waters of a flood.

STEVEN

I'm impressed! I didn't know we had such scholars in our midst.

LETICIA

Mandatory – undergraduate – humanities - courses. I was bored senseless.

STEVEN

Do we have any other examples of agreements with a Higher Power? Perhaps more upbeat examples?

WANG

There were agreements between the Greeks and their Gods. Athena agreed to help Odysseus return home to Detroit.

TRISH

Hermes agreed to give Odysseus the moly plant so he could overcome Circe and remain macho.

STEVEN

And the Romans?

KAMAL

There was Romulus and Remus, the children of Mars, who agreed to invent Chinese food.

TRISH

And Pluto who, after agreeing to ferry the dead across the River Styx, discovered ice fishing.

STEVEN

Okay, I deserved that.

WANG

Professor, what does all this have to do with science?

>   (Before he can answer, STEVEN gasps, grabs his chest,
>   and staggers backwards to his desk.)

TRISH

What's wrong?! Are you okay?!

>   (The students start to rise to go to STEVEN'S aid but
>   he waves them off, takes a pill from a bottle in his
>   pocket, and places it under his tongue.)

STEVEN

I'm fine. Really, I'm fine. Just a slight heart condition.

>   (STEVEN holds up the bottle.)

Digitalis.

>   (STEVEN rests a few more moments, and then returns
>   to the podium.)

All right. Let's go on. This is outside the box. What if you believed you discovered a really important scientific fact about existence that you suspected a Higher Power wanted disclosed, but not just yet, and instead of waiting for the Higher Power to come to you to make a "Do Not Disclose" deal, you just mentally asked for a sign that you were on

STEVEN (Cont.)

the right track with your discovery, that it was truly profound, that it was so profound it would result in guaranteed fame and fortune, and that the Higher Power understood you did not want fame and fortune because you considered it absurd under the circumstances.

TRISH

I'm sorry Professor, but I don't have a clue as to what you're talking about. What secret? What Higher Power? What sign? What do fame and fortune have to do with it?

(A cell phone rings. COREY jumps up and pulls his from his pocket.)

COREY

I'm sorry everyone, I thought I turned it off.

(COREY looks to see who's calling.)

It's my Dad. I have to take it.

(COREY exits.)

STEVEN

You know, Trish, sometimes even Professors get twisted up in their own rhetoric. I'm often not sure myself what I'm talking about. My wife says it happens more than often. Let's see if I can do better.

(STEVEN goes to the blackboard, picks up a piece of chalk, and starts to write. COREY returns, ashen.)

COREY

My Dad says all the heads of state have awakened from their comas and are resuming their duties.

(BLACKOUT)

(END OF ACT I)

ACT II

Scene 1

SETTING: The Office/Conference Room.

AT RISE: The room is empty. Then, the Professor and students file in, chatting as they go. They take their positions at the Conference Table. The blackboard is blank. The calendar shows February.

STEVEN

Good morning! I hope you all had pleasant weekends. Mine was spent in a titanic life and death struggle with a gopher and I regret to inform you the gopher won. The Championship Belt will be presented to the gopher by Kermit The Frog at The Wind In The Willows Inn on Penny Lane next Thursday should you wish to attend. With that little detail aside, I suggest we begin.

KAMAL

Professor, before we do, you said in December you thought it was essential for the meek to inherit the earth. Could you expand on that a bit?

STEVEN

Yes, that's what today's discussion is all about: humans embracing humility. But there are many different kinds of

STEVEN (Cont.)

humility, and many different paths to it, and we are going to discuss one in particular today: cosmic humility.

WANG

Which is?

STEVEN

An awareness so vast it would change people's perception of themselves and of life on earth.

LETICIA

Don't be modest. Say what you mean.

STEVEN

(laughing)

Fair enough. Basically, I want to explore whether there are techniques, patterns of thought really, that people can use to step outside themselves in order to see themselves more realistically; and to do it in the context of the wider world around them and their place in it.

LETICIA

To achieve "Cosmic Awareness," I gather. But why?

STEVEN

I'm going to leave to another day "why" humans should achieve Cosmic Awareness. But for today, I want to consider

STEVEN (Cont.)

"how" to achieve it. I'd like to begin with a quote from a good friend of mine, which I think beautifully captures the essence of it:

(He reads.)

"Indeed, we have already sensed our capacity if not longing for Cosmic Awareness lying in the grass under a blazing night canopy, sitting on the beach as the sun slips into the sea, standing on the edge of an immense Grand Canyon, hiking above a lush river valley dappled with shafts of sunlight, and yearning for intelligent life elsewhere in the universe."

TRISH

That's lovely. I assume you're going to tell us how to achieve Cosmic Awareness?

STEVEN

No, you're going to tell me. I want you to give me examples of things people can do to not only heighten awareness of the cosmos, but to bring to consciousness the staggering inverse dimensions of the subatomic world and the endless expanses of time. If you can think it, you can say it.

LETICIA

I would urge all men and women to let the starry sky enfold them, to visit the natural wonders of the world to experience

LETICIA (Cont.)

the awe and majesty of nature, and to place themselves in context from time to time by looking down at themselves from a mile up, then a thousand miles up, then ten thousand miles up, and then as far as their imagination can soar.

KAMAL

I would ask people to take a long look at NASA's photos of the Earth and the Moon taken from the orbit of Saturn that painfully inform the heart of man's ineffable loneliness in space.

WANG

Maybe Cosmic Awareness would help people understand that those on Earth who waved at the camera when the photos from Saturn were taken, could just as easily been waving goodbye as hello.

COREY

I would want people to understand that we have one of the more pedestrian view seats in the theater of the universe.

STEVEN

What do you mean by "pedestrian view seats?"

COREY

We may be stunned by the profusion of stars, gas and dust in our night sky, but it pales in comparison to what the

COREY (Cont.)

night sky would look like from an asteroid racing past an exploding star, or from a rogue planet transiting above the plane of the Milky Way, or from a Jupiter-size planet near the galactic center.

TRISH

I believe people should pay more attention to the messages we get from nature every day reminding us of the terrible fragility, and ephemeral nature, of our existence.

KAMAL

Which are?

TRISH

Hurricanes, earthquakes, volcanoes, tornados, meteors, forest fires, floods and tsunamis. To us they are background noise but their more profound, underlying meaning must be made manifest.

STEVEN

You know what's interesting? In all of human history, natural disaster has been the only force compelling changes in human behavior that man was willing to accept with equanimity and resignation rather than rage and riot. I wonder if we're going to have to take that road again.

LETICIA

I think people should remember that our uniqueness is a two-edged sword. However special we may be in intellect and achievement, we still "take" from nature, "make" into things, and "waste" in landfills and incinerators.

WANG

But that's the natural order of things!

LETICIA

No, it isn't. All other organisms contribute to the cycle of life in their birth, death, decay, regeneration and restoration. There is no waste in nature, yet humans are awash in garbage. I don't think there will be sustainability for man without conformity to the circularity of nature.

STEVEN

This is pretty heavy stuff. Anybody want to take a break?
 (No one answers.)
Okay, let's continue.

TRISH

I think people should acknowledge we are the only species given the choice of consciously avoiding overpopulation, and our advancement of family planning and birth control should be broad and deep.

WANG

I believe people have to stop thinking of Earth as a planet and start thinking of it as a lifeboat; a lifeboat in which ours may sadly be the last, great, gluttonous generation to task the planet before the tipping point.

STEVEN

For myself, I think that our egocentricity, our obsession with ourselves, our total preoccupation every moment of every day with who we are and what we do to the exclusion of the wider world around us, is the ultimate barrier to Cosmic Awareness.

COREY

I would ask our religious leaders to de-emphasize if they will those aspects of the faith that encourage our egocentricity and sense of entitlement, and emphasize those that help us fathom our true role in nature and our responsibility for both the despoliation and restoration of our habitat.

LETICIA

Nicely put!

STEVEN

Any other contributions? Ideas?

(No one has has anything further to add. But they

STEVEN (Cont.)

preen at each other as though what they just offered
was more than impressive.)
This explosion of ideas is exactly what I was hoping to
accomplish with this seminar. Just light the fuse and step
aside. You guys did great!

KAMAL

Do you have any additional ideas, Professor?

STEVEN

A couple, maybe. I don't think people can fully appreciate
Cosmic Awareness without understanding where humans
stand in the hierarchy of existence. The universe expresses
itself in many forms such as space-time, radiation, galaxies,
stars, planets, moons, atmospheres, continents, oceans,
"life," molecules, atoms, and particles, and we are putting
at risk the form of expression that is us.

WANG

You said you had a second idea?

STEVEN

Yes, and it's one that causes me great concern. I believe we
are at war with an enemy we have faced before, but not with
such dire consequences because this time our civilization
hangs in the balance. We are at war with ourselves and

STEVEN (Cont.)

200,000 years of genetic compulsion, only now we have to change the way we think in order to know how to act.
(STEVEN let's that sink in.)
Very well. I am Professor Steven Hamcke and I declare this first session of the Cosmic Awareness Club closed!

(BLACKOUT)

(END OF SCENE)

ACT II

Scene 2

SETTING: The Control Room.

AT RISE: The room is dark and empty, lit only by the glowing and blinking lights of the computers and laptops. MYRA enters and flips on the light switch. HALE, BRYAN and GLENN follow her into the room. BRYAN and HALE check their computers while GLENN and MYRA tidy up the table. Then, MYRA, HALE and GLENN sit down while BRYAN remains at his desk. The calendar shows February.

BRYAN
(looking at his computer)
All quiet on Earth, but there's a chance of afternoon showers on Mars.

MYRA
Very funny! Any chance the rain on Mars will cause life to flourish there just as a cooling planet protects it here?

BRYAN
I can't see Flourish from here but Fertility looks dry as a bone.

MYRA

Okay, so why must Earth suffer an officious intermeddler on climate while Mars gets a free pass?

GLENN

I wouldn't exactly call favorable trends in global warming "suffering."

MYRA

Fair enough, but what is causing these trends?

BRYAN

Nothing. There are no trends. It's the data. It's just bad data. Garbage in, garbage out. The only question is, is it our data or our predecessors' data?

HALE

We've checked and double-checked ours and it's accurate. And there's no way the entire environmental science community that preceded us could have been so off the mark for so many years with its data. I don't buy it.

MYRA

Which leaves us nowhere. The trends and coincidences for every environmental problem we've identified are favorable. Why? Think outside the box.

BRYAN

Martians.

MYRA

Not that far outside the box.

GLENN

Natural causes. The planet has some self-healing mechanisms we know nothing about. We always start from the premise we know how the earth works. Maybe we don't.

HALE

Maybe it's some outside force, and I'm not talking about aliens. Maybe the solar system is a single organism that can heal its own parts and we're just not aware how it does it.

MYRA

That's pretty far-fetched.

HALE

Here's something far-fetchier. You know how in 1998 astronomers discovered that the expansion of the universe was accelerating. Well, gas cools as it expands. Maybe the acceleration of the expansion of the universe reached a point where everything in it is cooling, including Earth.

BRYAN

Maybe the earth itself is expanding and cooling and we haven't noticed it. When was the last time anyone checked its circumference?

MYRA

Well, we can go on like this all day but I'm not sure how productive it will be. Why don't we return to our work for the Intergovernmental Panel. Glenn has been looking at sustainability issues. Any trends stand out in either the problems or the solutions?

GLENN

As always, the problems are global warming, overpopulation, and resource exhaustion. They present a particularly difficult problem for cities. Yet cities hold out the best hope for making advances in sustainability.

MYRA

Why is that?

GLENN

Because that's where more and more people are concentrated and it's people that create sustainability. This will be especially true if we're going to build cities over and higher.

HALE

So, what are the solutions?

GLENN

Cities need to be designed in accordance with the circularity principles of nature.

HALE

Which are?

GLENN

The use of all available techniques to ensure that incoming resources are designed for "next use" and not "end of life," and buildings perform the functions of trees.

BRYAN

Now, that's clever. Clever and impossible, of course.

GLENN

Not if we maximize use of wind, solar and geothermal energy; treat waste as a resource; exploit the efficiencies of living and working in the same neighborhood; eliminate commuting time and transportation pollution; and use rooftops for farming.

BRYAN

I stand corrected. Did you see any trends?

GLENN

Yes, the reported number of people who are moving to the cities has been badly underestimated. A recent report said

GLENN (Cont.)

in the U.S alone, half the population will live in eight states in 20 years. I assume most of them will live in cities even as cities renovate themselves and grow taller.

MYRA

Nice work, Glenn. I'll report our discussion today to the Intergovernmental Panel: that is the part of our discussion dealing with sustainability, and not the part speculating on what might be causing the earth to cool. We'll keep that to ourselves and put it in the "To Be Considered Later" file. If there's nothing else, why don't we return to our accelerator experiments.

BRYAN

Wait! Let me mention something before I forget. You know how sometimes people contact us and have recommendations of other uses we can make of the collider?

GLENN

Yeah! Like that idiot who suggested we remove all the equipment from the ten-mile ring and turn it into a raceway for remote-controlled mini-cars.

BRYAN

Right. Well I wanted to tell you about an email I received that makes an even weirder suggestion.

MYRA

Who sent it?

BRYAN

I don't know. When I tried to respond with our usual: "Thank you for your interest in our lab and the work we do," my email came back undeliverable.

HALE

What caught your eye?

BRYAN

Well, the guy said . . .

MYRA

Wait! How did you know it was a guy?

BRYAN

He signed his email "Steven." Anyway, he urged us to conduct an experiment that would make use of the Scientific Method which requires, as you know, the construction of a hypothesis, the testing of the hypothesis by experiment, the drawing of a conclusion from the data, and the communication of the results.

MYRA

It sounds like he knows a bit about science. What was his hypothesis?

BRYAN

That time can move in opposite directions in the same universe.

GLENN

Terrific! Fantasyland here we come.

HALE

What's the experiment?

BRYAN

He wants us to use the collider to send a question out into the universe.

MYRA

What's the question?

BRYAN

"Is anybody there?"

GLENN

How are we supposed to do that?

BRYAN

By firing protons in Morse code.
> (They consider this a moment, then break out in bemused laughter at the absurdity of the idea.)

(BLACKOUT)

(END OF SCENE)

<u>ACT II</u>

Scene 3

SETTING: The Office/Conference Room.

AT RISE: The Professor and students are engaged in conversation at the conference table. The blackboard is blank. The calendar shows March.

TRISH

. . . that may be true but I really didn't understand what you were driving at when you talked about making a deal with a Higher Power that involves fame and fortune.

STEVEN

I've been thinking about that too and overall I think I would give myself a "D" minus for the effort. If you like I could try again, but this time I would start from a different perspective.

TRISH

Please do.

STEVEN

Let me begin with something of a ghoulish question. In dealing with a Higher Power, under what circumstances might the reward you ask for be death? It's a question that has long fascinated me.

WANG

Obviously, if I had an excruciatingly painful terminal illness.

STEVEN

Of course.

COREY

Perhaps if I were a soldier and dishonored my country with cowardice and everyone knew it.

STEVEN

Yes.

LETICIA

Perhaps for the hundred and one reasons people commit suicide, whatever they are.

STEVEN

Certainly, that would fit. Now, let me put the question into the context of our previous discussion. But please don't forget, this is just a thought experiment, nothing more.
(STEVEN goes to the blackboard.)
Step One: A scientist believes he or she has discovered a profound secret about existence.
(STEVEN writes "Discovery" on the blackboard.)
Step Two: Part of that discovery is the realization that a Higher Power will eventually want it disclosed.

STEVEN (Cont.)

(STEVEN writes "Disclosure" on the blackboard.)
Step Three: The scientist also knows that with disclosure fame and fortune will be certain.

(STEVEN writes "Fame and Fortune" on the blackboard.)
Step Four: The scientist hates the limelight and strongly believes that, under these circumstances, any desire for fame and fortune would not only be ridiculous, it would be embarrassing. Stating it another way, the desire deserves to be extinguished by the discovery.

(STEVEN writes "Ridiculous" on the blackboard.)
Step Five: The scientist wants no part of fame and fortune and asks, thinks, prays if you want, for two things: that no disclosure of the discovery be made until he or she is dead, and for a special sign confirming the discovery is correct.

(STEVEN writes "Death" and "Special Sign" on the blackboard.)
I trust I have made myself perfectly obscure.

TRISH

You certainly gave it a shot. But let me ask: Why are we discussing this in a science seminar?

STEVEN

(returning to the podium)

I just don't think you should have a discussion about science without discussing a Higher Power as well.

COREY

Professor, could we return to something you said last session? You said you wanted to leave for another day the question of "why" humans should strive to achieve Cosmic Awareness. Could we get into that?

STEVEN

Sure. But first we need to determine if humans are "capable" of achieving Cosmic Awareness. It may be possible because we do have a record of achieving higher perspectives during our history. Can you give me examples?

COREY

Sure. We thought our planet was flat, but learned it was round.

WANG

We thought the earth was the center of the solar system, but learned the sun was the center.

KAMAL

We thought stars were uniformly distant, but learned galaxies race away from us in an expanding universe.

STEVEN

Indeed, one day we may even discover that not everything has a beginning and end. But in every past instance, our well-being did not depend on adopting a new, and higher, worldview. That may no longer be the case. Why do you suppose that is?

LETICIA

Because problems such as overpopulation, environmental degradation, and resource exhaustion beset humanity and many believe these problems are unsolvable.

STEVEN

They may be if our vision remains static. But if it does not, if it can rise to a higher plane, where might that lead? Stating in another way, what is the logical next step up in human perspective?

LETICIA

Cosmic Awareness?

TRISH

Just so you know, I believe these problems are unsolvable because humans are preprogramed by their genes to act in a certain way. A leopard can't change its spots. Humans can't stop acting the way they do, even if they wanted to.

COREY

It may go deeper than that. I think it's possible the constants in the universe, such as entropy and the masses of fundamental particles, are such that the kind of intelligent life they allow may not be able to evolve beyond its age of technology.

STEVEN

But for the moment, let's say it's not hopeless. Why might that be?

LETICIA

Well, theoretically, our species has the intellectual capacity to secure its future on this planet if it can change the way it thinks: if perhaps it can achieve what you've been referring to as Cosmic Awareness, and truly grasp its place in the universe.

KAMAL

Isn't that where humility comes into play: cosmic humility? As counterintuitive as it seems, humans may have to embrace their monumental insignificance before they can act positively and effectively to combat existential threats.

COREY

I think what he's saying is as long as we think we're special, we're fucked.

STEVEN

But what happens after Cosmic Awareness is achieved? What comes next?

LETICIA

Great effort and enormous sacrifice. Cosmic Awareness will be needed to make them both bearable and desirable.

STEVEN

What kind of effort and sacrifice are you talking about?

LETICIA

Full mobilization. To truly fight the coming ravages of overpopulation, environmental degradation, and resource exhaustion, humans will have to go on the equivalent of a war footing and conserve energy on a massive scale.

WANG

I agree. Maybe fifty years ago we could have gotten away with the kind of bullshit Band-Aids we're applying now, but those days are gone for good. We've let things slide too far.

KAMAL

I'm sorry, but I think you're being far too pessimistic. I know for certain humans are the most adaptable species on the planet, and I believe we will find a way to cope. Besides,

KAMAL (Cont.)

who says things are really that bad? Who says the naysayers are right?

STEVEN

Exactly! Why should we start with the assumption humanity's problems are unsolvable? You should have to prove it. In fact, you're going to have to prove it to me.

KAMAL

Why? If we think the problems are solvable, why should we try to convince you otherwise?

STEVEN

Because "Devil's Advocacy" is a great teaching tool that will either confirm your beliefs or reveal the flaws in your thinking.

COREY

So, you want us to argue the position that things are awful regardless of our personal beliefs?

STEVEN

Basically, yes . . . Oh, God! Please, not again.

 (STEVEN grabs his chest. A pantomime ensues: STEVEN can't find his pills; the kids rush to help; STEVEN signals frantically toward his desk; LETICIA finds his pills; STEVEN puts one under his tongue.)

LETICIA
You know, that was the last pill. Have you more?
(STEVEN gestures toward the desk.)

(BLACKOUT)

(END OF SCENE)

<u>ACT II</u>

Scene 4

SETTING: The Control Room.

AT RISE: BRYAN, HALE and GLENN are at their desks looking at their computer screens. MYRA is at the table signing papers. A test of the system, which everyone ignores, is underway and we can hear the PINGS and see the particle showers just as before. The calendar shows March. The test comes to an end and the screen goes dark.

GLENN

(turning from his computer)

Everyone ready to go?

MYRA

Sure.

(MYRA puts away her papers and the guys join her at the table.)

Anyone go to a good seafood restaurant recently?

(No one answers.)

Well, you better get a move on if what I read about fisheries collapsing is true. It's pretty dire. Bryan, what does your research show?

BRYAN

There was a study done in 2006 predicting all seafood fisheries will collapse by 2050. "Collapse" is defined as a 90 percent depletion of the species' baseline abundance.

MYRA

I think we can see why this project is Confidential. If we publicly reported the trends we've discovered so far, the lid would come off the pressure cooker and all efforts at conservation would cease. God only knows what it would do to fisheries. Overfishing would go through the roof.

BRYAN

The study also concluded that the loss of marine biodiversity worldwide is profoundly reducing the ocean's ability to produce seafood, resist disease, filter pollutants and rebound from stresses such as climate change and overfishing.

HALE

I heard the collapse can also affect human health if depleted coastal ecosystems become vulnerable to invasive species, disease outbreaks, and toxic algae blooms. Is that right?

BRYAN

Yes. And there have been other studies on the subject. In 2016, according to the U.N. Food and Agricultural

BRYAN (Cont.)

Organization, 85 percent of global fish stocks were overexploited, depleted or recovering from depletion.

MYRA

Overfishing isn't the only driver of the collapse, is it?

BRYAN

No, there are many other causes that contribute to the problem. High levels of consumption, external inputs like fertilizers, the adoption of new technology, the introduction or removal of species, disease, and global climate change all play a part.

HALE

I'm curious. What countries are most responsible for overfishing?

BRYAN

Japan, China, the U.S., Indonesia, Taiwan, and South Korea all make the "shame list;" especially as regards tuna. Other overfishing heavy hitters are Peru and Chile.

GLENN

Christ, are there any solutions at all? Is it even possible to find solutions?

BRYAN

There are, actually, because of the ocean's unique ability to recover from insults quickly. But at this time, the solutions being tried are just a drop in the ocean, excuse the pun.

MYRA

Is there a point of no return?

BRYAN

If species are not pushed too far down, recovery can be swift, but there "is" a point of no return where recovery is unlikely.

HALE

What other solutions are proposed?

BRYAN

For one, the aggressive enforcement of laws prohibiting the exploitation of endangered fisheries and the pollution of surrounding seas.

HALE

For another?

BRYAN

The sequestering of 30 percent of the oceans into marine protected areas including those close to shore where most activity occurs.

MYRA

Now comes the big question. Are there any favorable trends?

BRYAN

Yes, one, and it's impressive. Very, very recent studies show fish stocks are recovering far faster than anyone thought possible.

MYRA

I'm at a loss, fellas. I simply don't know what this means.

HALE

Hey, Bryan! Have you heard anything further from the guy who suggested we fire protons in Morse code?

BRYAN

Yes, and I found what he had to say rather interesting although his ideas have no basis in science and, strangely enough, he admits it.

HALE

What do you mean?

BRYAN

(taking a paper from his pocket)
Here's what he said, and I quote: "I do not have any scientific evidence to support my hypothesis but have arrived at it by induction, inference, and intuition. Therefore, the inquiry

BRYAN (Cont.)

is quixotic. But the experiment to test the hypothesis is so effortless and cost free it is worth trying."

GLENN

What else does he say?

BRYAN

He says his hypothesis is based entirely on the concept of "reciprocality," which is variously defined as "present or existing on both sides; each to the other; mutual," or "corresponding but reversed or inverted."

MYRA

Sounds like two sides of the same coin. It also sounds like yin yang, which, as I understand it, are complementary forces that interact to form a dynamic system in which the whole is greater than the assembled parts.

BRYAN

He claims reciprocality pervades the universe and that it is virtually impossible for man to think of a concept that does not have its other side.

HALE

For example?

BRYAN

You need up to have down. They are both directions. You need cold to have hot. They are both temperatures. You need life to have death. They are both states of being. You need fast to have slow. They are both speeds. You need good to have evil. They are both moral judgments. He says these examples are but a tiny few of the inversely related, opposite reciprocals that comprise the universe.

GLENN

Okay, but so what?

BRYAN

Well, he goes on to ask why, if the universe allows reciprocality, it cannot allow a portion of the overall universe to contain matter and energy that is separate from, and reciprocal to, the matter and energy in our portion of the universe, but is virtually undetectable because time there moves in the opposite direction of time here.

HALE

I'll tell you why? Because it's bullshit! There is not a shred of evidence to support the existence of a reciprocal universe.

BRYAN

I know. He also refers to our share of the overall universe as "our universe" and the reciprocal share of the overall universe as the "reciprocal universe."

MYRA

Do you think his theory has any merit?

BRYAN

I think the odds against it are colossal. But I'm fascinated by the fact his theory reflects both yin yang and the definition of reciprocality. As he points out, our universe and the reciprocal universe are present or existing on both sides, each to the other, mutual; that the reciprocal universe is corresponding but reversed or inverted; and that our universe and the reciprocal universe interact to form a dynamic system in which the whole is greater than the assembled parts.

GLENN

Neat theory. Bad science. Anything else?

BRYAN

Just a thought that intrigues me. If his theory allows our universe and the reciprocal universe to communicate, it might mean we can communicate in real time rather than, for example, the eight plus years it would take to send a signal to, and receive a signal from, our nearest star; assuming, of course, that star had a planet with intelligent life orbiting around it.

(BLACKOUT)

(END OF SCENE)

ACT II

Scene 5

SETTING: The Office/Conference Room.

AT RISE: STEVEN is erasing the blackboard. COREY and KAMAL are examining the certificates on the wall. TRISH is on her cell phone and WANG and LETICIA are writing at the table. The calendar shows April.

STEVEN

(going to the podium)

Shall we begin?

(They all join him at the table.)

I'd like to open today by offering congratulations to you for a job well done. My hopes for this seminar are being fulfilled in our free exchange of ideas, our exposing of contradictions, our challenging of shop-worn beliefs, our rapid-fire dialogue, and our testing of different learning techniques. I can't wait to read your theses.

LETICIA

I know I speak for everyone, Professor, when I say the pleasure was all yours.

181

STEVEN

(laughing)

It was! It really was! Anyway, putting such high praise aside, I would, as I said last time, like to take the "Devil's Advocate" approach to learning out for a spin.

KAMAL

That means we have to convince you the world is a mess even though we don't believe it?

TRISH

Some of us believe it!

STEVEN

Yes, but not quite. I don't want you to say, "Here's why the world is a mess." I want you to say, "Here are the things that happened that set the stage for the world to become a mess." Then, I'll decide if you've made your case.

COREY

How far back do you want us to go?

STEVEN

The Big Bang, of course. I want the perspective of deep time.

WANG

Well, that certainly limits the inquiry. Any other modest requirements?

STEVEN

Yes, I want it to be a race. I want you to go as fast as you can, each in turn. As always, I'm looking for spontaneous declarations to reveal things you know that you don't know you know. I'll fill in if someone hesitates. I'll start: the Big Bang 13.8 billion years ago.

COREY

The universe expanded and cooled,

KAMAL

Light was released to stream toward our eyes even though we wouldn't exist for many billions of years.

TRISH

Stars, galaxies and planets formed and hydrogen and helium evolved into the myriad elements we know today.
    (WANG hesitates.)

STEVEN

Human beings represent the most complex arrangement of those elements to date: blindly stitched together by evolution, blindly following the laws of nature.

WANG

Whether that universe was set in motion by a quantum emergence, a multiverse, a Big Crunch, or some other agency,

WANG (Cont.)

it seems clear that humans are an infinitesimal, unimportant speck in an indifferent universe and that their survival depends on acceptance of that reality.

LETICIA

Our own eyes tell us the only thing in the solar system that cares about us is us.

COREY

The earth doesn't care what's on its surface, and all the other planets and moons in the solar system attest to that. That is probably true for all of space.

KAMAL

So, if there are solutions to our problems they must come from us, for us, and for all the other species we have placed at risk.

TRISH

That is why we need to develop Cosmic Awareness: because that way lies hope. We cannot fix problems without admitting truths.

WANG

One truth might be that humanity's most significant contribution to evolution will, in the end, be nothing more

WANG (Cont.)

than the transfer of the fossil fuels of the earth from the ground to the air.

LETICIA

Another truth might be that humans as evolved are destined to be an interim species: why else why would their technology have gotten so far ahead of their enlightenment?

COREY

Another truth might be that humans, the most adaptable species on the planet, are simply ill equipped conceptually and psychologically to adapt to the storm that is coming.

KAMAL

We know the planet has limits and never before have so many people been in harm's way. During prior warming periods, there was no one around.

TRISH

Never before in perhaps 65 million years has the climate changed so fast even taking into account random pauses in warming. Never before have humans engaged in such an existential, planet-wide experiment that could redound catastrophically to their detriment.

(LETICIA hesitates.)

STEVEN

Basically, the human business model has changed. We can no longer migrate, hunt, gather, fish, sow, reap, build, produce, reproduce and exploit without limit or consequence.

LETICIA

Many biologists believe that, absent a massive asteroid strike or tremendous geological activity, humans will be the cause of the sixth mass extinction in the last 450 million years.

COREY

The possibility exists that in the next 100 to 1,000 years, the combination of human overpopulation, environmental degradation, and resource exhaustion will cause a massive kill-back of species on this planet, including our own.

(KAMAL hesitates.)

STEVEN

Notice he said kill-back, not extinction, though many species will indeed go extinct.

KAMAL

Right. No one can predict who or what will survive in such an environment.

TRISH

Perhaps there are genetic mutations that have occurred or are occurring now in various species that, over time, will allow them to endure higher temperatures.

WANG

And consume less food and water.

LETICIA

And breathe higher concentrations of methane and carbon dioxide.

(COREY hesitates.)

STEVEN

No one knows.

(There are no more contributions.)

Very well! It does seem the world is a mess for very sound historical reasons. But if I may, and this is just because I'm curious, what would you do to clean up the mess?

COREY

I would create a ten-year plan to entirely phase out the emission of greenhouse gases in our country and to minimize the contamination of its land and seas.

KAMAL

I would create a new generation schooled in the religion of best environmental practices from childhood.

TRISH

I would participate in as many international organizations as possible working to limit the climate change and contamination underway.

WANG

I don't think we should be so naïve as to believe the U.S. can tackle climate change on its own, but perhaps we can hold the line in the hope others will catch up in time.

LETICIA

I would try to educate people to understand that consumption begets production which begets pollution; and that the use of endless, mindless consumption and production as cure-alls for economic ills is self-defeating. As regards the preservation of a healthy planet, less is more.

COREY

There's a secondary benefit. A reduction in endless, mindless consumption and production will slow resource exhaustion and perhaps buy time for renewables to predominate.

STEVEN

For myself, I would try to educate people to accept that sacrifice is necessary to achieve the higher good of a livable planet. Developed nations must cut back on the standard of living they enjoy. Developing nations must postpone

STEVEN (Cont.)

some of the standard of living they seek. Otherwise, we are just admitting that even if cutbacks and postponements are necessary, we would rather party on until nature does them for us, disastrously.

(BLACKOUT)

(END OF SCENE)

ACT II

Scene 6

SETTING: The Control Room.

AT RISE: MYRA, GLENN, BRYAN and HALE are seated at the table talking. The screen is filled with a cascade of particle showers, just as before, and it will continue for awhile. The calendar shows April.

MYRA

(gesturing towards the screen)

. . .and that's why astrophysicists at the University of Cambridge asked us to rebroadcast these results.

HALE

What time frame?

MYRA

Three years ago on December 16th, between 2:31 and 15 seconds and 2:47 and 43 seconds, p.m.

HALE

I'll be interested to see what they found.

MYRA

Right. Well, you'll be pleased to know the Intergovernmental Panel has asked us to resurrect the "Ass Backwards Project,"

190

MYRA (Cont.)

but only for one particular subject they are deeply concerned about.

GLENN

And that is?

MYRA

The effect of advances in technology on society. Apparently, they feel an unorthodox approach will better reveal trends.

BRYAN

You don't have to farm it out to someone for study. We can do it right here, right now. Conclusion: We're screwed, and are being screwed.

MYRA

Do you really believe that?

BRYAN

Absolutely!

GLENN

Me too.

HALE

Me too.

MYRA

Why, for heaven's sake?

BRYAN

We'll show you. Here's the solution: A law needs to be passed that forces technology companies to split-off affiliates or lines of business or percentages of business.

GLENN

Here's the problem: They have become too big, too influential, too unmonitored, too politically powerful, too gate-keeper dominant, and too "Big Brotherish."

HALE

Here's another solution: We need to create new economic models to equitably distribute employment and income. The economic models must repurpose technology away from consumption and toward reduced working hours and a wider distribution of available jobs.

BRYAN

And perhaps provide meaningful and fulfilling free time by subsidizing individual efforts to improve the environment or help people in need.

GLENN

Here's the problem: In a world where peoples' sense of self-worth is derived from their work, millions of unemployed

GLENN (Cont.)

displaced by technology will be wandering around feeling insecure and wondering what the hell to do with themselves.

HALE

Another problem? As long as technology keeps encouraging consumption, global warming will run amuck.

MYRA

Well, that's disheartening. Do you see any favorable trends?
(MYRA'S inquiry is met by silence.)
Okay? Let's change subjects for now. Has our "fire protons in Morse Code" friend had anything further to say?
(The screen goes dark.)

BRYAN

Yes, I received a new email yesterday. He speculates that we cannot cross from our universe to the reciprocal universe without ripping the fabric of space-time.

GLENN

A typical science fiction plot point.

BRYAN

But he does believe that we can communicate with each other where physics is uncertain: beyond the speed of light, within black holes, or below the size of the atom.

HALE

So, that's where use of our particle accelerator comes in! All our work is below the size of the atom. We deal with sub-atomic particles. Protons are sub-atomic particles.

GLENN

Fair enough! I'll concede that physics is uncertain beyond the speed of light, within black holes, and below the size of the atom, and we have absolutely no idea what goes on there: what laws apply. But using them as a method for communicating is a stretch.

MYRA

Well, we're not entirely in the dark below the size of the atom where uncertainty prevails. We may not know why the quantum world is uncertain, but we can at least use probabilities to make fairly accurate predictions about the future.

GLENN

Still, to me, uncertainty and a reciprocal universe don't match up.

BRYAN

Really? How about this? We are uncertain if a multiverse exists. Our universe and the reciprocal universe make two. We are uncertain if black holes contain wormholes allowing travel elsewhere in the universe. Perhaps they just allow

BRYAN (Cont.)

communications between the two universes. We are uncertain if dark matter and dark energy exist. Perhaps they simply originate in the reciprocal universe. And we are uncertain if anything can travel faster than the speed of light. Perhaps a message from the reciprocal universe to us can start out faster than the speed of light and arrive slower than the speed of light.

HALE

Very neat! But why does he recommend we fire protons in Morse code? How would that even work?

BRYAN

He says he knows we can program the computers to time the firing of the protons: that we can actually fire them in any sequence we want. He says we should be able to fire them in a Morse code sequence to spell out a message. He admits it's primitive but believes simplicity is necessary.

HALE

Why is simplicity necessary?

BRYAN

I have absolutely no idea.

MYRA

Why Morse code? Why not Swahili? Or Pig Latin?

BRYAN

I have absolutely no idea.

GLENN

Did he have anything else to say?

BRYAN

Yes. He said that if there is both our universe and a reciprocal universe, perhaps they influence each other like two cable cars passing each other where the one coming down lifts the one going up and the one going up slows the one coming down.

GLENN

Yes, but cable cars are connected by a cable. What connects the two universes?

BRYAN

I have absolutely no idea. Maybe time.

HALE

But time is ephemeral. Insubstantial.

BRYAN

Is entropy? What do you think?

HALE

I have absolutely no idea.

GLENN

Wait a minute! He says time in the two universes is moving in opposite directions and that the universes are somehow connected. Do they pass by each other like cable cars, or do they pass through each other?

BRYAN

I don't know. But I like the idea that an entire invisible universe is passing right in front of me.

MYRA

What else did he say?

BRYAN

He says because of this connection between the two universes, when our universe accelerates from its Big Bang, the reciprocal universe accelerates from the end of its expansion. And when our universe decelerates toward the end of its expansion, the reciprocal universe decelerates towards its Big Crunch. These effects are true for both universes and in neither case is gravity a factor. The influence of one universe on the other outweighs it.

GLENN

So, he comes down on the side of the Big Crunch theory. No beginning and end: just two parts of one universe recycling forever. Did he have anything else to say?

BRYAN

Isn't that enough?

(BLACKOUT)

(END OF SCENE)

ACT II

Scene 7

SETTING: The Office/Conference Room.

AT RISE: The Professor and students are gathered around the conference table looking at spectacular posters of galaxies and stars which we can see when they pick the posters up. The Professor is unsteady on his feet and will remain so. The blackboard is blank. The calendar shows May.

STEVEN

Let's get started.

(They take their positions.)

Today is our last session and because you've earned it I'm declaring it "Potpourri Day." You can ask me anything you want and I will, as the saying goes, cast pearls of wisdom before simulated swine.

KAMAL

Good, because I want to ask about a couple of things mentioned earlier. Someone said they suspected the constants in the universe are such that the kind of intelligent life they allow may not be able to evolve beyond its age of technology. Another person said humans might be fated to be an interim

KAMAL (Cont.)

species else why would their technology have gotten so far ahead of their enlightenment. Let's say for the moment that all that is true. Is there no hope at all?

STEVEN

If I may make a wild ass guess, perhaps there is. Perhaps we will be helped over the rough patch, what I like to call the inflection point, by aliens. The inflection point is where intelligent life begins to destroy itself because its technology has gotten too far ahead of its enlightenment.

WANG

(chagrined)

Really, Professor? Aliens?

STEVEN

Well, not exactly the kind of aliens you might imagine. Here's my speculation. You don't have to understand the details, just the overall idea. First, if time can move in opposite directions in the same universe, it implies there may be a reciprocal universe with matter and energy in it that we can't detect. Second, there may be intelligent life in the reciprocal universe that is far more advanced than we are. Third, that intelligent life will want to help us get past our inflection point the same way our prior universe helped

STEVEN (Cont.)

them get past theirs, and if they don't help us now we won't be around to help them at their next inflection point.

WANG

Professor, I swear I have no idea what you're talking about.

STEVEN

It's simple. Just remember four things: inflection point, reciprocal universe, intelligent life, and willing assistance. I will now entertain additional questions.

WANG

One more on this subject, please. How would intelligent life in the reciprocal universe communicate with us?

STEVEN

By the simplest means possible I should think: at least in the beginning. Obviously, they could communicate with us any way they pleased in incredibly sophisticated ways, but to start, I think they would want to keep it simple and for us to send the first message so they could be sure we were seeking contact and their answer would not scare us witless.

LETICIA

Changing topics for the moment, Professor, what do "you" think are the great unanswered questions in physics?

STEVEN

Corey, you can help me with this. I would first say our inability to unify general relativity, which governs the very large, and quantum mechanics, which governs the very small, into a single theory of quantum gravity.

COREY

I would say not being able to explain the existence of dark matter and dark energy, which comprise 95.1 percent of the total mass-energy of the universe. Ordinary matter comprises just 4.9 percent.

STEVEN

I would also say not knowing how many dimensions the universe has above and beyond the three we know, plus time.

COREY

Probably failing to grasp why there is more matter than antimatter in the universe.

STEVEN

Not knowing for certain what causes the quantum wave function to collapse, but we won't go into that.

COREY

And perhaps not fully understanding "spooky action at a distance," but we won't go into that, either.

TRISH

My turn. What is "inflation?" I keep hearing about it.

STEVEN

Corey?

COREY

It's a theory that says there was a tremendous burst of the expansion of space an infinitesimally small amount of time after the Big Bang.

TRISH

Why did it occur? What does it do?

COREY

We don't know why it occurred. But if it hadn't occurred, we wouldn't have the universe we see today and we wouldn't be here.

TRISH

Did it do anything else?

COREY

There are physicists who believe the universe would not appear to be the same in every direction without inflation.

TRISH

Is it possible the universe could be the way it is without inflation? Could there be some other cause?

STEVEN

Not that we know of, but if you allow me to fall back on my wild ass guess that a reciprocal universe might exist, and I cannot emphasize strongly enough the words "wild ass," then maybe as our universe expanded from its Big Bang, the influence of the reciprocal universe caused the flattening, structuring, distribution and uniformity of our universe, rather than inflation.

TRISH

Do you really believe a reciprocal universe can exist?

STEVEN

I believe . . . Ow! Ow! God dammit!
>(STEVEN grabs his chest. We can see he is in agony. He staggers backward to sit on the edge of his desk.)

TRISH

Professor, are you okay?
>(STEVEN searches frantically in his pockets for his pills but to no avail. The students rush to his side.)

COREY

Leticia, get his pills! In the desk!
>(LETICIA races to the desk, desperately searches the drawers, piles file after file on the desktop, and finds nothing.)

LETICIA

There are no pills here! I can't find anything!
>(STEVEN lets out a massive groan and stumbles to the conference table where he collapses and brings a chair down with him.)

TRISH

Oh, my God! Kamal, get help! Please hurry!
>(KAMAL races from the room.)

WANG

Professor can you hear me? Can you hear me?
>(STEVEN is unmoving. WANG checks his pulse, then listens for his breath, then does them again. He shakes his head.)
I think he's dead!

TRISH

>(tearful, regarding STEVEN fondly, then surprised)
Is it possible he's smiling?

WANG

No, that's a pain grimace

LETICIA

>(drifting toward the table, reading a document)
This can't be real!

TRISH

What is it?

LETICIA

This computer printout was in his desk. It's a list of all the heads of state who went into comas at the same time.

WANG

He kept a list. So, what?

LETICIA

It's dated three days before the comas occurred.

COREY

(pausing, reflecting)

Is it possible, is it possible, that the deal between the scientist and a Higher Power wasn't hypothetical; (Beat) that the special sign the scientist asked for from the Higher Power was a warning shot across the bow of dictators and demagogues; (Beat) and that we were not brought here for a seminar but to bear witness?

(BLACKOUT)

(END OF SCENE)

ACT II

Scene 8

SETTING: The Control Room.

AT RISE: The room is empty and dark except for the glow of computer lights. HALE enters, and turns on the overheads. He is followed by BRYAN, MYRA and GLENN. While MYRA is preoccupied by HALE, BRYAN rushes to the desks and brushes rubber ducks off them into a wastepaper basket as fast as he can. Then, they all sit at the table. It is dark outside. The screen is dark. The calendar shows May.

MYRA

I apologize for calling you in on a Sunday evening. The Intergovernmental Panel was scheduled to issue its report on Friday but leaks have forced it to advance its press conference to tomorrow morning. They have asked us to please double check our findings one last time, which is exactly what we did last week, and to answer three questions which they may or may not release to the public. I wanted to be sure we had a consensus.

GLENN

What are the questions?

MYRA

First, are humans capable of changing how they act in order to combat global warming, overpopulation, and resource exhaustion? Second, can advances in human technology successfully combat those threats? Third, do the trends we discovered confirm the planet is cooling and, if so, why?

BRYAN

In a nutshell: Probably not . . . Possibly, but it's a long shot . . . Yes, but we don't know why.

MYRA

Let's flesh that out a bit but keep it simple. And remember, nobody says we're right.

HALE

I'll take the first question: As was suggested before, it appears humans are genetically predisposed to ruin their habitat. Unless they can somehow change the way they think, they are intellectually and psychologically incapable of turning a distant threat into an immediate response that requires sacrifice. So, humans are probably incapable of changing the way they act, at least as far as the three threats are concerned.

GLENN

On the other hand, it is possible that advances in human technology can overcome the threats, but it's a long shot because it's a foot race between how fast technology can ramp up versus how fast the three threats can double down. There is no way we can know the outcome in advance.

BRYAN

And, yes, it does appear the planet is cooling. We have no idea why and can only speculate, which is not good science. Worst of all, we have no idea if it will continue.

MYRA

Anybody disagree?

(No one speaks.)

Okay, we have a consensus. Anything else?

HALE

Yes, I'm curious. Bryan have you heard anything further from the Morse code guy?

BRYAN

I have. He sent me an email at home but I didn't know it was there because I hadn't checked my Inbox for several days.

GLENN

Anything interesting?

BRYAN

I think so. He asserted that the influence of our universe and the reciprocal universe on each other, over time, caused the flattening, structuring, distribution and uniformity of the other, making inflation unnecessary.

GLENN

Did he acknowledge the contradiction between his theory that our universe would stop expanding and start contracting, and the commonly accepted fact that our universe is not only expanding, the expansion is accelerating?

BRYAN

He did. He conceded it was a tricky problem. But he believes we have not yet detected the slowing of the acceleration of the expansion of our universe, and we can never detect the slowing of the deceleration of the contraction of the reciprocal universe. How's that for a mouthful?

MYRA

Hard to follow. Anything else?

BRYAN

Yes. He answered the great unanswered questions of physics. He said you can unify general relativity and quantum mechanics across the universes, rather than within them. He said dark matter and dark energy are just matter and

BRYAN (Cont.)

energy in the reciprocal universe, indirectly perceived. And he said there are only eight space-time dimensions: four in our universe and four in the reciprocal universe.

HALE

That's not all of the unanswered questions, by any means.

BRYAN

No, he had other answers. He said matter and antimatter are balanced when you take into account both universes. He said opposing time in both universes collapsed the quantum wave function in each. And he said opposing nanosecond time made "spooky action at a distance" an illusion in both.

MYRA

Well, it's original thinking, I'll give him that. Is that it?

BRYAN

No, he then wrapped it all up in a nice, neat package. Let me read what he said:

> (BRYAN pulls a paper from his pocket and starts reading.)

"So, if our universe is almost 14 billion years old, and there is a reciprocal universe influencing our universe and everything in it, it is possible we have about 14 billion years

BRYAN (Cont.)

left to get to the end of the expansion of our universe or, stating it another way, we are one quarter of the way though our cycle of Big Bang, expansion, contraction, and Big Crunch, and the reciprocal universe is three-quarters of the way through its cycle of Big Bang, expansion, contraction, and Big Crunch making it about 42 billion years old."

(BRYAN stops reading to let that sink in.)

Now, here comes the punch line: "And if the reciprocal universe is about 42 billion years old, and intelligent life there has survived its age of technology, that life would be incredibly advanced and possibly waiting for a signal from us that we are mature enough for contact. Thus, the question: 'Is anybody there?'"

HALE

Myra, do you think we should try the experiment? Aren't you the least bit curious?

MYRA

Let me give you my views on that in the clearest possible terms. The proposed experiment is truly speculative and I will not have this lab become the laughing stock of the scientific community. I will not endanger our funding. I will not impair our prestige. I will not embarrass the board. And I will not cause all of us to be terminated. So that you understand me

MYRA (Cont.)

in no uncertain terms, if anyone tries it I will fire him on the spot. Now, having said that, I need to get home.

GLENN

Me too.

(MYRA and GLENN collect their belongings and leave.)

BRYAN

That sounds like a threat.

HALE

She's not kidding.

BRYAN

I agree. Let's give it a try!

HALE

Are you out of your mind? Why?

BRYAN

Because I'm more afraid of not satisfying my curiosity than I am of getting fired. It's why I became a scientist.

HALE

What do you think the odds are of making contact with intelligent life in a reciprocal universe?

BRYAN

One chance in a billion, or worse.

HALE

Then why?

BRYAN

That one chance lights my fire.

HALE

How would you go about it?

BRYAN

I'd program the computer: first, to fire the protons in a sequence that asks the key question in Morse code, and second, to evaluate the particle showers for an answer in Morse code.

HALE

How long would it take to set that up?

BRYAN

I've already done it.

HALE

Jesus, Bryan! You're really asking for it!
    (HALE mulls things over.)
I just don't know . . .

BRYAN

Come on, Hale, have some balls or leave the room and I'll do it myself. I'll cover our tracks. Myra will never know. Turn out the lights so no one can see we're here.

> (HALE wrestles with the idea. With a sigh he gets up and turns out the lights so only the glow of the computers illuminates the room.)

HALE

Did you turn off the universal distribution function?

BRYAN

Damn, I forgot! That's all we need: A thousand witnesses.

> (BRYAN goes to his computer and types in commands.)

There! Ready? Okay, here we go . . .

> (BRYAN types additional commands into his computer as he speaks.)

Is . . .

> (The computer PINGS "Is" in Morse code.)

Anybody . . .

> (The computer PINGS "Anybody" in Morse code.)

There . . .

> (The computer PINGS "There" in Morse code.)

Keep your fingers crossed.

> (BRYAN stands up and he and HALE watch the screen from opposite sides of the room. The screen remains

BRYAN (Cont.)

dark for a few seconds, then lights up with static. A few seconds later we see five particle showers, just as before, and then the screen returns to static. Five seconds go by and then we see a small white line appear in the center of the screen. Slowly, slowly, it grows larger and larger in both height and width through the static until we can discern it is comprised of four components. It grows ever larger until we can discern the components appear to be words. The words finally resolve into clarity and say, "YES. WE ARE HERE.") Oh, my God!

(BLACKOUT)

(END OF PLAY)